The Song of the Sword

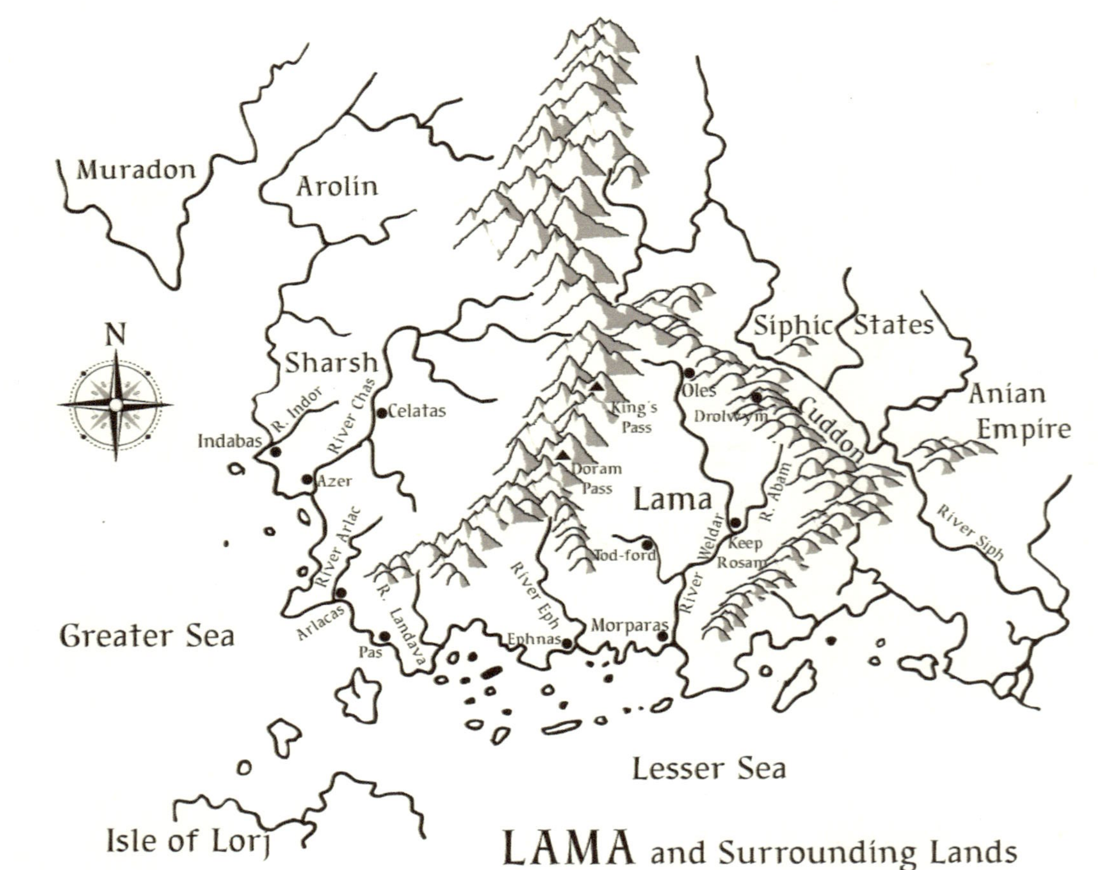
Muradon
Arolín
Sharsh
N
R. Indor
River Chas
Celatas
Indabas
Azer
River Arlac
Arlacas
Pas
R. Landava
Greater Sea
Isle of Lorj
King's Pass
Doram Pass
Lama
Oles
Drolwym
Cuddon
Siphic States
Anian Empire
R. Abam
Keep Rosam
River Weldar
Nod-ford
River Eph
Ephnas
Morparas
River Siph
Lesser Sea
LAMA and Surrounding Lands

THE SONG OF THE SWORD

STEPHEN BROOKE

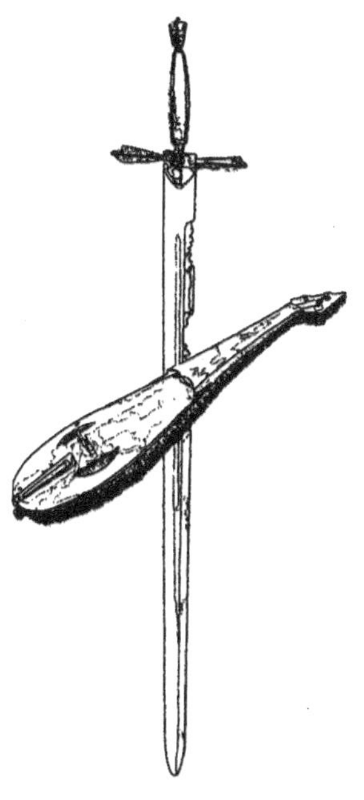

Arachis Press 2013

He knew now with certainty what he had suspected: Donzalo would be not an ordinary man but a man of destiny.

ISBN 978-1-937745-11-0

Arachis Press
4803 Peanut Road
Graceville, FL 32440
http://arachispress.com

The Donzalo's Destiny epic fantasy
by Stephen Brooke consists of four books:
I. The Song of the Sword
II. The Shadow of Ask
III. The Sign of the Arrow
IV. The Hand of the Sorcerer

OF SONS: THE FIRST TALE

1

Tall mountains, tall battlements and a tall man upon them – here, on the border of his realm, Lareth looked to the East. Odd, he mused, that he be in this place. Odd and ironic, for only a generation earlier his father had wrested this land and this castle from old Duke Paren. Now, joined by marriage to that same family, he awaited word making their alliance more permanent. The East would be opened for trade, opened, perhaps, for expansion.

From the battlements, the king had watched his messenger ride in. This arrival meant a report at last, be it good or bad: at worst, the death of his daughter in childbirth. Well loved and youngest of his children, Lareth had regretted the necessity of her marriage to that Eastern clod. Yet that was ever the fate of princesses, to wed where policy best was served.

But now the news, of whatever sort, would be known for here approached the man, escorted by Lord Radal.

"Your highness, the messenger," announced the dark nobleman. A travel-worn knight dropped to one knee before his king.

"Speak."

"Sire, the best of tidings: the Lady Lomela has given birth to a son. Both she and the baby were healthy when I departed Castle Rosam."

The king smiled, but his look of concern remained.

"Excellent news. We thank you – Sir Blen, isn't it? You must be quite weary after such a journey. Go find yourself a meal and a bed.

"Lord Radal, remain please. I have matters to discuss with you."

Radal tossed the man a small purse and dismissed him with a nod. He stood, awaiting his king's word, in the shadow of the stone arches.

Lareth turned from his adviser, looking again to the East.

"Now must we heed the Oracle. Its warning was clear enough."

"Too clear to ignore, my king."

"And Cars is ever a true oracle. You know we cannot change what is to be, Radal."

"Yet, sire, we must try."

"We must try. Yes, we must try." The king spoke quietly now, almost to himself. "There can be no threat to the child nor to his future.

"So we act," he announced, his decision made. "You will be our ambassador, Radal. Take the usual gifts to the parents and the family, and take whom and what you need to remove the danger."

Again gazing eastward, he paused a moment. "Our grandson shall be heir to Borrago, despite the pronouncements of Cars. Go now."

Lord Radal bowed and left his king, brooding still upon the battlements.

~ ~ ~

Another castle, another man. From his seat at the high table, Count Borrago surveyed the feasters filling his hall. It was large, the Great Hall his father had built, yet it overflowed. Then, with the air of a thoroughly satisfied man, he leaned back and addressed his brother.

"Events could not have turned out better, eh? Our alliance with Sharsh is firmly cemented and I have an heir."

"It's good that your boy settled down and fathered a legitimate son at last," answered the burly Paren, a man given to plain speech.

"Indeed. There are enough bastards about this place. Bolos has been chasing chamber maids and serving wenches since he had legs to run on."

His eyes fell on his younger son, seated at a side table where he listened intently to the tales of a group of travelers. "I sometimes wish Donzalo would run after a woman or two."

"You always judge him too harshly. I would be pleased that he is not like his brother. And he dotes on the child, already."

"I'm glad of that. He and Bolos have never gotten along. Perhaps the baby will bring them closer."

Sir Paren considered this a moment. "I rather doubt it," he said, looking up at the massive ceiling beams, hewn of oak from the forests near his own manor. "Bolos seems to have little interest in his offspring, or in his wife for that matter. I hear he has scarce touched her since their wedding night."

"Apparently, they touched enough," chuckled Borrago. "It's a shame, though, that he and Lomela don't seem to care for each other. I fear she thinks him a complete lout."

"You must admit he can be."

"Yes, and she can put on her airs as well as any other western lady. Then she turns around to become a giggling girl, which is just as bad!"

"Well, that's youth for you. I certainly put up with enough from you when we were boys. And," Paren, ever tolerant, continued with a smile, "she is very young yet. No older than Donzalo."

"Both their heads are filled with the same childish romantic nonsense. There's too much of this Sharshite chivalry about."

"It's the way of the times, Borri. Even quite sensible and serious fighting men try to act the gallant these days.

"Now what's this commotion over by the doors?"

Borrago straightened up to take a look. "Another arrival, I suppose. Go see who it is, will you?"

"No need. Here they come. Ah, they're from Sharsh."

~ ~ ~

"A rather uncouth assemblage, sir."

Radal glanced at his youthful aide. "The most powerful Eastern nobles are here." His tone was even, matter-of-fact, that of patient teacher to pupil. "They are not to be sneered at."

"The count rises to greet you, my lord. He shows great respect."

"Also his shortness. He stands so as not to be dwarfed by those seated around him, especially his bear of a brother. Remain with the gifts and keep your silence."

The Sharshite lord, a tall, dark, lean man, his stylishly embroidered black tunic gray with the dust of the road, approached the dais to make a deep and graceful bow.

"To his grace, Borrago, Count Rosam, greetings from his royal highness, and your faithful brother, Lareth. I bear the best wishes and congratulations of Sharsh's king and people for Lord Bolos and Lady Lomela at the birth of a son, and gifts for the child." He waved the aide forward. "Here be –"

The count broke in. "It is custom here to present the gifts on the naming day. That will be two days hence, sir."

Radal nodded and gestured for his man to withdraw. "Then, my lord, may I present myself?"

"By all means," spoke Borrago, settling back into his chair. He knew this man, though, and his reputation. Why might such an envoy come to him?

Showing no signs of being disconcerted by the count's direct manner, the Sharshite continued. "I am Radal, Knight and Lord Councilor of Sharsh. In the name of King Lareth, and acting as his personal ambassador, I bid good health to you, my lord, and to all this company, and humbly request your hospitality."

Neither failed to note the stir Radal's name had created among those present. Borrago suspected that the man enjoyed his notoriety.

"Welcome, Lord Radal, to County Rosam and the free lands of Lama." Borrago could not resist pointing out that he and his guests recognized no overlord. Nor did he – nor Radal, for that matter – fail to appreciate the political advantages to be gained by mentioning it before his peers. Too many had concerns about this apparent alliance with Sharsh.

"And welcome to our celebration. But, surely, you are worn with travel. Sir Paren, will you see to our guests?" The look he gave his brother clearly said, "I do not trust this fellow. Keep an eye on him."

The envoy bowed, the ghost of a smile on his thin clean-shaven face. "We thank you for your hospitality, your grace."

"Feel free to join us once you have settled in, Lord Radal," invited the count. "If you are too tired, my brother will have something sent from the kitchens."

"I fear, my lord, fatigue will prevent our presence."

"Until the morrow, then. We ride to the hunt early, should you wish to accompany us. For now, I bid you good night."

"This way, sir," said Paren, and led Sharsh's delegation from the hall.

2

"You didn't return last night."

"By the time I finished with the Sharshites, I was in need of sleep." Paren smiled and added, with an air of mock apology. "You know I'm not as young as I used to be."

"Ha. You could never keep up with me."

"I never wanted to."

"Thank you for attending to them. Any problems?" queried the count. "I see none chose to ride with us this morning."

"It would have been surprising if they had; the way from Sharsh is long and weary, and they rode fast and hard. I am astonished they managed to get a delegation here at all before the naming ceremony.

"Ah the hounds have a scent." Paren shielded his eyes and looked toward his brother's pack.

"Another coyote, no doubt. Let the others ride ahead; I would talk with you."

The knight reined in his horse, a sturdy mount of Anian lineage, bred for the hunt and the hills. Trotting beside his brother, he spoke. "This Radal's presence concerns you?"

"Yes, Parri. It makes no sense for such a man to serve as ambassador." He shook his head. "No sense at all."

"Because of his position?" asked Paren. "Or because of his, uh, reputation?"

"Because of the effect his reputation might create here. Lareth must feel he has some strong reason to risk offending me and the other nobles."

"He fears someone. Why else send an assassin?"

"More than an assassin – a sorcerer."

"I do not trust those who deal in magic."

"Nor do I," agreed Borrago. "But by all accounts he is loyal to his king."

Paren was silent for a moment. "You do not think he would strike at you?"

"At this time? Lareth is not a fool."

"No. Perhaps he only seeks to safeguard the child."

"Perhaps. Some of our guests are, indeed, less than reputable. Did Lord Radal ask after any of them?"

"Not by name. He seemed more interested in the family." Paren raised his head. "It sounds like the chase is on."

The brothers galloped to the top of a ridge. Below was the hunt, in full pursuit of their prey.

"A prairie wolf, isn't it?" asked the count, pointing into the broad, shallow valley.

"Aye. I haven't seen one here in years," answered Paren. "Your hounds have no experience with such prey. You may lose some."

"Can you make out that horseman in the lead? I know your eyes are better than mine."

"Guesare."

"The Cuddonian? He's a bold one." Borrago's tone expressed admiration.

Paren chuckled. "But one of those less than reputable fellows you mentioned."

"True. Let's ride to the kill."

This was the heartland of County Rosam, a patchwork of farm and forest spread upon the rolling hills. The two noblemen angled down the slope to intercept the hunting party.

"The wolf has turned to fight," called Paren, "yet none of your pack has courage enough to close with him."

"They were bred for intelligence," the count retorted.

"Look. Guesare has arrived."

They watched the hunter approach the snarling, harried wolf, ringed by baying hounds. He passed at full gallop, loosing an arrow from the saddle.

"He handles a bow like an Easterner."

"The wolf is down. Now my pack is on it!"

The brothers, and the rest of the hunt, had caught up with the Cuddonian. Dismounting, the master of hounds beat his charges back from their kill.

"A huge beast, my lord," he reported to Borrago.

"Is the skin worth saving?"

"I think not, sir. 'Tis badly torn."

"It was your kill, young Guesare. Do you want a trophy?"

"Dispose of it as you will, Cousin," answered the young man, lounging in his saddle. "I have many such at home."

The count raised an eyebrow, then nodded. "Take the head, Master Saj, and let the hounds have the rest." He wheeled his horse. "Gentlemen, you may continue the hunt without me. Sir Paren and I return to the keep."

~ ~ ~

"What kin is Guesare to us? A third cousin?"

"I believe so. It's difficult to keep Mother's family sorted out."

"He seems half an Anian."

"Some nobles of the Cuddon do have Ani blood. None in his line, though, as far as I know. Of course," Paren admitted, "there are many things I don't know. He doesn't look Ani, anyway."

The count and his brother were riding up a winding dirt road to Castle Rosam, pasture land on either side. On the highest point of a ridge, overlooking the River Weldar, stood the keep. Less than two miles below, the Weldar was joined by the waters of the Abam. It was one of the most important sites, strategically and economically, in all of Lama.

"His familiarity with me borders on contempt."

"In the marches, we are accustomed to that."

Paren looked wistfully down at River Abam. More than twenty leagues up its stream lay his home, a simple but well fortified manor near the borders of the Cuddon. At heart, he was a farmer, and ill at ease with the politics of Castle Rosam.

"It's good to have you here, Parri, and the Lady Thara, too. We miss a woman's touch in this pile of stones."

"You have Mother." Paren's smile was full of mischief. "Isn't she the mistress of the manor?"

"She's more interested in entertaining young minstrels than running a household."

"I don't suppose Lomela's any help?"

"The girl has been very careful not to assert herself, but she will, in time. I've been watching her build a loyal circle." Borrago gave his brother a meaningful look. "She's very much her father's daughter."

"Bolos will need such a woman by his side."

"If he will listen to her."

They passed through the last of three concentric stone walls, each higher than the one before, to enter the keep. Built on a leveled hilltop, most of the structures here – the great hall, barracks, stables – were of wood. In the center, however, rose a stone tower, Castle Rosam's last line of defense.

Dismounting, Paren gestured toward a trebuchet standing in one corner of the spacious yard. "Why do you have that antique here?"

"That's Donzalo's toy," laughed the count. "He can lob a stone right into the river. Well," he continued, "most of the time. I must admit it's cheaper than playing with a cannon."

"Does he still have some notion of us starting our own foundry?"

"Yes. The boy is a dreamer. Here, lad, take care of our horses." Borrago handed the reins to a groom. "We won't need them again this day."

~ ~ ~

Perdos and Percos were ill at ease.

"What if we were seen?" asked the older brother.

"Someone might suspect," added Percos, the younger.

"Many visitors have called here," the Lord Radal assured them, "and with so many coming and going all through this keep, none will make special note of you."

"We've been keeping our eyes open, sir," said Perdos. "Do you want a report?"

Radal managed to conceal his contempt. "Later, perhaps." These thugs were useless as spies. What he needed now was muscle. "Do you know young Donzalo?"

"Donzalo?"

"He's not important."

"We've been getting close to Bolos."

"Hmm. What does he think of his brother?"

"He holds him a weakling."

"Yes." Percos nodded his head. "Bolos bullies the boy."

"And what is your opinion?"

The two looked at each other. "I've never thought about it," Percos admitted.

"Me, neither," agreed Perdos.

"But he seems a decent enough young fellow."

"Harmless."

Radal openly sneered. "I need him truly harmless. Can you make him so?"

"Here?" wondered Perdos. "In his father's own manse?"

"Most accidents do occur at home," Percos pointed out.

Perdos gave the Sharshite what he thought a shrewd look. "Pruning the family tree, eh?"

"You might say so, but don't. It is none of your affair."

"It shouldn't be difficult to get the boy alone. He is trusting and keeps no personal retainers about him."

"Over the wall, you think?" Percos asked.

"He might fall into a cistern," suggested Perdos.

"Whatever," interrupted Lord Radal, "but nothing too subtle. It must seem an obvious accident. Any death," he pointed out, "is bound to draw suspicion to me."

"Ah." Percos had an insight. "Otherwise, you'd just poison the lad and be done with it."

The Sharshite was amused. "There is hope for you two. Gold, also, when you are successful." And a life of blackmail later, thought Radal. It would be useful to have these fools in Bolos's inner circle.

"You may leave me now."

~ ~ ~

"Good afternoon, Grandmother. Lomela? They let you out of bed?"

"I let myself out of bed. It's been near two weeks! My attendants would have kept me there forever. I think they fully expected me to nurse the child, too!" The young mother grimaced. "But the Lady Vibola rescued me and found a wet-nurse."

"Grandmother, you spoil her. Father would not approve."

"Borrago has picked up too many peasant ways in this land," spoke the old woman, from her seat near the fire. It was early spring, and still cool. "Unlike his father, who was a true gentleman of Sharsh." She looked up at the tall, gawky young man. "Come sit by me, Donzalo."

"You speak of the Count Ros, my lady?" inquired Lomela. "What was he like?"

"I wish you would call me Grandmother."

"Very well, my Lady Grandmother," she impishly replied.

"Behave," warned Donzalo, "or we shall start addressing you as 'Princess.'"

"Saucy boy. You should learn your place." The Lady Lomela tossed back her long, wavy hair. She was young and spirited, and knew she was attractive, though no great beauty. "I would know of the man if my son is to be his namesake."

"Ros was the youngest of old Duke Paren's four sons. The other three died in battle against your grandfather's forces." Lady Vibola nodded toward the girl. "But Ros had been sent to aid in the struggle against the Ani here in the East."

"Did the duke die, too?" asked Lomela. "There is disagreement among the histories I have read."

"No, he escaped the taking of his keep. Paren stayed here a time after that." She stopped for a moment, lost in her memories. "An ugly, bandy-legged, little fellow he was," she continued, "with a great, bristling mustache. Borrago rather favors him."

"Didn't he go east?" prompted Donzalo.

"Don't interrupt," Lomela told him.

"He traveled to the Siphic city-states and became a condotierre. Remarried and raised a whole other family there, I understand.

"Ros looked little like his father. He was tall and handsome and very gallant." The old woman let her gaze linger on Donzalo for a moment. He seemed so much like his grandfather. "But a man, still," she mused, "with all the good and ill that brings."

Lomela was suddenly serious. "Was your marriage arranged?"

"He sought my hand. Oh, there were politics involved, to be sure, in its winning. My parents had many doubts as to this adventurer who'd come calling." The old woman smiled. "I helped them make up their minds."

"A minstrel should tell your tale!" Lomela decided. "Let's put one on it."

"None here are good enough," objected Donzalo." Our court does not attract talent."

"I think we may have just the man among our guests," stated Lady Vibola. "I shall invite him to join us later."

3

The naming ceremony takes place tomorrow morning, my lord," Radal's aide informed him. "Feasting in the evening."

"No other celebrations?"

"It is considered a holy occasion, sir, to be kept solemnly. There will be a tourney and fair the next day."

"They do follow the Kamation rites?"

"Largely, sir. They seem a zealous people."

"They are a fanatical people."

"My lord?" The young man was puzzled.

"Their religion and their fight for independence have so intertwined that they see themselves as a holy nation, surrounded by infidels. The years of Anian domination saw to that."

The aide pondered his words. "My lord, doesn't that make them, well, dangerous?"

Radal laughed. "It does, indeed. That, my boy, is why we are here." The nobleman paused a moment. "We should have known when the gift-giving takes place."

The younger man nodded cautiously.

"But that is more my fault than yours. We both were forced to leave Sharsh too hurriedly." Radal's voice took on a serious note. "There is a lesson for both of us there." His eyes returned to the dispatches spread before him.

"Yes, my lord. Will you have further need?"

"I think not. You've some place to go?" He glanced up. "A girl, perhaps?"

"An invitation from the Lady Lomela. You know, my lord, we were friends at court."

"Of course. It got you this assignment."

"Yes, my lord, I was aware of that." Slightly embarrassed, the aide went on. "She wants to introduce me to her circle. The count's younger son will be there, and some minstrel from the east."

"Guesare?" The envoy took sudden interest. That name had occasionally popped up in his dispatches, often linked to questionable occurrences.

"I believe that's the name, sir."

"Go. But later, Jobareth, I want a full report on your evening. Do you understand?"

"Yes, sir."

Radal smiled to himself. He could not have asked for a better spy than this trusting young fellow.

~ ~ ~

"Bolos drinks much too heavily. Can't you say something to him, dear?"

"He is far past listening to his old uncle."

"Aunt Thara! Uncle Paren!" Donzalo was hastening after them, down the covered walkway that led toward their suite.

"What is it, child?" asked Lady Thara.

"Some of us are getting together in Grandmother's chambers. You are both invited." He paused for breath. "The Lady Lomela will be there, and a new minstrel."

"Oh, Donni, you know I'm not at ease at such gatherings."

"I think we will be retiring, boy."

"You're welcome if you decide to join us." Donzalo was disappointed, though this response had not been unexpected. "Good evening, Aunt Thara." He nodded toward Paren. "Uncle." The young man turned abruptly and hurried away.

"Are you certain you don't want to go?" Paren asked his wife. "You love music."

"Not in your mother's company. I couldn't take an evening of her looking down her nose at me."

"She never understood why I loved a plump little peasant girl." He hugged her. "And I still do."

"Donni's a sweet boy," Thara remarked. "It – it pleases me to think our son might have grown to be like him."

For a moment, both savored the bitter-sweet taste of memory.

"Hmm, yes," spoke Paren. "He will be our heir, I suppose, and reeve of the manor when I am gone. We should have him come stay with us."

"He could be your squire."

"Donzalo would learn little of knighthood at my side."

"But much of running a manor."

"I'll speak to Borri." He smiled at his wife. "It would do us all good."

~ ~ ~

"Here he comes."

"Act natural, now."

"Good evening, my lord."

Donzalo laughed. "No lord am I."

"Fool," Percos admonished his brother. "It is Master Donzalo."

"A lordling, then, and just as good. Lad, will you have a drink with us?"

"Why do you not drink with my brother?" asked the bemused youth. "Are you not his friends?"

"Lord Bolos dove too deeply into his cups and will not come up till the morn," the younger brother explained. "Won't you join us? We've, um, a full keg downstairs."

"Near the cistern," snickered Perdos.

"I thank you, no. I am expected by the Lady Vibola."

"Let the old woman wait. We have an excellent wine."

"From Sharsh," Perdos added.

"Yes, Sharsh – and a very good vintage," his brother agreed.

"Twenty-two."

"Twenty-two? That's not any good," objected Percos.

"Oh, of course. Twenty-three, 'tis. I had forgotten."

"I haven't the time, gentlemen." Donzalo brushed past them. "And I would thank you to speak more respectfully of my grandmother." He quickly vanished around a corner.

"You certainly ruined that. Vintage of Twenty-two, indeed!"

"It was all your fault. You insulted his granny."

"What do we do now?"

"Grab him after his party."

"And throw him over the wall!"

Perdos thought briefly. "We should have masks. Someone might see us."

"Let's go get them. And let's sample that wine, too."

"Idiot."

~ ~ ~

"What have you there, Jobareth?"

"A book, my lady. I thought to bring a gift for our hostess."

"She can not read." Lomela looked the slim volume over. "Not your poetry? You've had it printed?"

"There are three presses operating now in the capital, and the cost of printing keeps going down. Soon, everybody will be able to publish a book."

"I do not think Lady Vibola would understand your poems. She would not even understand the courtly language in which they are couched." She took his arm and confided "I read to her often, and her tastes run to the most lurid of romances.

"Come, let me present you. You might as well bring the book." She led the young Sharshite across the room, to where her grandmother-in-law reposed on a centrally placed divan.

"Lady Vibola, this is Master Jobareth Nafal, a gentleman of Sharsh and aide to the Lord Radal."

"My lady." He bent to kiss her hand. The older woman gave the younger an impish look.

"I like this one, Lomela. What have you there, young sir?"

"It's a book of his poems," the girl told her, taking it from his hands. "I shall read them to you later, but I must warn you that they are dreadful."

"Why doesn't the gentleman read some for us?"

Lomela feigned horror. "Oh, Grandmother," she moaned, "don't encourage him!"

"I would be honored, my lady."

"But not now, I think," said the older woman, smiling benevolently. "Lomela will want you to meet her friends."

Lady Vibola's suite of rooms, of paneled pine and draped with tapestries, were the largest private quarters in Castle Rosam. She had appropriated them after the count's wife had died and he moved into a small, spartan space in the tower. Her friends and favorites could gather here, as they had this evening.

Some of those attending were regular visitors, residents of castle or town. Other were guests, come for the naming celebration. Lomela introduced her friend around the room.

"Here's Donzalo, arriving at last," she told him.

"He's a tall one," commented the Sharshite.

"Yes," agreed Lomela. "I suspect he'll fill out and look like his uncle in a few years."

"By the way, my lady, please don't introduce me as 'Master.' It's 'Lector' since I finished at the university."

"Very well," the young woman laughed. "Donzalo will be jealous; his father would not permit him to study abroad." She showed sudden, rather exaggerated, puzzlement. "He's coming over. Now which of you should I present to the other? He's of the more noble family, but you have found a title and position."

Jobareth gave her a suspicious look. "I feel you are poking fun at me, Lady Lomela. But, truly, in his home he takes precedence." Nafal was well-schooled in protocol.

"Very well." She turned to her brother-in-law. "Master Donzalo Rosam, may I introduce Lector Jobareth Nafal?"

"Pleased." He extended his hand but looked at Lomela. "My lady, how is the baby?"

"He is fine, Donzalo, and well cared for, or I would not be here." Her voice took on a note of exasperation. "My servants thought it most frivolous to leave the child on the eve of his naming day."

"That's not surprising, Lomela, I mean, my lady." He turned back toward her friend. "Lector, huh? We must talk later. Very pleased to meet you – I should pay my respects to Grandmother."

"Yes, pleased." An amused Jobareth watched the gawky Laman leave, pushing his way through the crowded room.

"Donzalo can be terribly rude at times but he means nothing by it. Please like him." Lomela sounded anxious.

Nafal nodded. "I already do. And I know the type well; the university is full of them. Including," he laughed, "most of the professors."

More seriously, he noted, "You like him a great deal."

Lomela seemed slightly flustered. "He's the only one in this dismal place with any culture," she replied, "the only one I can – talk with." She was finding it hard to put into words. "Oh, he's the only one here who understands me."

"Then he's a better man than I, my lady. I have always found you quite baffling."

"Humph. I've been around Lamans long enough to see through your courtly banter, Jobareth. Come, the minstrel is about to play."

4

Donzalo's long legs carried him along the western rampart. Behind him scurried two tall figures, heads covered with black cloths, eyes peering through ill-cut holes.

Though not the shortest way to his rooms, it kept him out of the mud and stench and noise of a lower route. And he liked the view here, high above the river and town. The boy longed to pass down the Weldar some day, to the great port Morparas and its university.

As he paused a moment, refreshing this dream, his shadows rushed him.

"Get his legs!" barked one, clamping a hand over the struggling Donzalo's mouth.

"Ow! He kicked me," complained the other. "Got him now."

"Over the wall with him!"

On three sides of Castle Rosam, the hill rose gradually and wide grassy spaces were left between the three concentric walls. Here, it stood steep and the lower battlements were little more than catwalks above a cliff face. He would fall a very long way.

Another figure suddenly joined them. Unlike their intended victim, this was a man who knew how to fight, and fight well. One assailant dropped from a blow to the face. The other let Donzalo loose and attempted to grapple with the newcomer, only to meet hard fists, two to his midsection, one – lower. So, that quickly, it was ended. Doubled over, he and his partner fled.

"Guesare!" the youth choked out.

"If my rebec is damaged, I shall be most unhappy," stated the minstrel, removing the instrument from its bag.

"Wh – what happened?"

"It seems, young kinsman, those ruffians meant to assassinate you." He looked his rebec over. "And nearly succeeded. But neither you nor my instrument," he decided, putting it away, "appears harmed."

"I thank you, sir." Donzalo was puzzled. "Why would anyone wish to kill me? I mean, I am nobody. Even I know that."

"You are third in line to the title of count. That makes you someone." The Cuddonian's mood became sober. "Let's get you to your quarters. I think we need to talk, you and I."

~ ~ ~

Jobareth knew better than to question his master about the two men – one limping – he passed outside their rooms. He hoped only to slip in unnoticed and find his bed.

Luck was not with him. "Tell me of your evening," ordered Lord Radal, "before sleep softens the memories."

"My lord, it was but a gathering of the more, um, sophisticated Lamans. Something of a welcome diversion in this dour land."

"The Lady Lomela is at the center of this group?"

"Near the center, sir. The count's mother holds that place, but the princess will, I think, be her heir."

Radal nodded. "Who made up the guests? Be thorough."

"A number were of the merchant class, my lord, either residing in the town or travelers who do business there. They are often more cultured than the nobles in Lama."

"Travel broadens one."

"Yes, sir. There was a sprinkling of noble visitors, some from the Cuddon. The Lady Vibola's family springs from those hills, I am told. Also, members of the local nobility, mostly young. They seem to revolve around the Lady Lomela."

The councilor considered this. "Not surprising," he said, almost to himself, and then asked, "what of the count's younger son? Donzalo."

"Oddly, sir," reported the aide, "most of his friends are townspeople. His interests are too scholarly, perhaps, for Laman noblemen."

"Then he holds little influence?"

"On the contrary, my lord. He seems Lady Lomela's closest friend in this place. Further, his circle includes many who may not be noble but have considerable wealth."

"Ah. There was a minstrel, you say?"

"More than one, sir. Two mediocre fellows currently at residence in the castle, and Lady Vibola's cousin."

"This Guesare of whom I have heard so much."

"Yes, my lord. His work is excellent, if somewhat old-fashioned. He insists on rhyming his lines and is somewhat free in his meter."

The Sharshite lord permitted himself a small smile. "He is, I understand, quite a fighting man."

"So they say, my lord, though he struck me as a bit frivolous. And, um –"

Radal noted his reluctance. "Continue."

"Well, I think he made a pass at me. Sir."

The nobleman openly laughed. "Feel flattered, Jobareth. That will be all." He looked down at his papers as his aide left.

Too bad, he thought, that this young fellow didn't share the Cuddonian's tastes. It would make him an even more useful spy.

~ ~ ~

"We only have suspicions as to who is involved. If the count acted now, we might never know the truth of them. But this we know: the king has gotten it into his head that you are a threat."

"Me? Why would Lareth think such a thing?"

"There is an explanation, and I may give it to you, in time. For now, I offer you my protection."

"There is an explanation for that, too, I suppose?" Donzalo's voice held more than a trace of sarcasm.

"Indeed there is, lad. Let us just say that my friends are Sharsh's enemies."

"That would include many people."

The Cuddonian smiled amiably. "Yes, it would." He stroked his curling, golden beard and looked about the young man's quarters. "You should be safe for the moment, but there will be other attempts. Lareth is not one to give up, nor is Radal."

"The ambassador? Oh, of course," Donzalo realized. "That is why he is here."

"You catch on quickly." The minstrel gave an approving nod. "His henchmen having failed, and you now being warned, he may act directly. And Lord Radal is a very dangerous man."

"They say he has skill in the black arts."

"They speak truth. I think, my boy, I should stick close to you from now on."

"Do you wish to stay here, tonight?" Donzalo's invitation came hesitantly. He occupied two small, cluttered rooms.

"I must go, but keep your door barred till morning. A thought," he added. "You might cultivate the envoy's young aide."

"Jobareth?"

"Aye. I doubt he is involved in any of this, yet he may prove a source of information. My own attempt to befriend him went awry." Guesare laughed ruefully. "I – misjudged the fellow."

"What of my assailants? I have suspicions as to their identity."

"As do I. Leave that for the morrow."

5

"Master Donzalo."

"Lector. Need help?"

"What place should the ambassador take in this procession?"

"I'm not sure." The young Laman had been assisting Sir Paren in his attempts at organization. "Uncle, where do you want Sharsh?"

Paren turned to them. "Lord Radal represents the child's grandfather. He should be up front with the family." He looked at Jobareth. "You could stay close behind him."

"I'll be a couple of rows back, too. Walk with me," suggested Donzalo, "and we can keep each other from being bored."

"Thank you, sirs. Uh, do you think this attire suitable?" He wore sober gray, a long Sharshite tunic, his sash minimally embroidered in white and yellow. "I confess, I did not expect so many bright colors this morning."

"You'll see more when we reach the town. We are not perpetually somber here."

"Gray is always appropriate," Paren felt. "Simple and unassuming."

"But you might suggest that Lord Radal not wear his accustomed black," added Donzalo, with a laugh. "It is spring, after all!"

"Yes, certainly. Good day, sirs." The Sharshite hurried away.

"I doubt Radal even owns anything that isn't black."

"He is very dark, himself," replied the knight. "I understand there's Southern blood in his family."

"His father was a mercenary from Lorj who rose high in Sharsh. Lomela told me that." Donzalo was struck by a sudden thought. "I wonder if the Wisest was so dark."

"I don't know, boy. Not all Lorjam are." Paren returned to his task. "Ho, there, where *are* you taking that cart?"

~ ~ ~

"Everyone walks?"

"Yes, my lord. It is considered more respectful."

"Very well," sighed Radal. "Let us be thankful the weather is still cool."

"Those who do not go on foot will be borne on litters. Perhaps, sir, I could arrange one."

"No, Jobareth, I shall walk. However, I will not wear a colorful costume."

"I did not – think you would, my lord," replied the aide, "but felt I should mention it to you." He sounded unsure.

"You acted correctly. I have hopes for you, young man."

"Hopes, sir?"

"There should be a permanent ambassador here. Not you, Nafal," he hastened to add. "You haven't enough age." Lord Radal placed his hand on the young man's shoulder, the long, dark fingers unadorned save his ring of office. "Some bland diplomat to hold the title, with you doing the real work – and reporting to me."

"The assignment would not be unwelcome, my lord," was Jobareth's thoughtful response. "This place is not nearly so bad as I feared."

"There are far worse posts, and it would be for but a while. We might as well go."

Although Castle Rosam had a chapel, most of the naming ceremony was to be held in the local temple, just above the town. Following a general blessing, they would proceed down to it.

First came the litter bearing Lady Lomela, all in white and rose, and her son, flanked by Bolos and a priest. Radal took his place in the second rank, beside Borrago and the Lady Vibola's litter. Behind them were Sir Paren, his wife – who had disdained a litter – and Donzalo. The count's son motioned for Jobareth to join him.

"Is it correct for me to be up here?"

"If anyone notices you, they'll just assume you have some role. Like the litter bearers." Donzalo waved his arm in their direction. "Or the bodyguards right behind us."

The Sharshite glanced at the four well-armed retainers. Further back, was a large group of kinsmen and noble guests, Guesare the minstrel among them.

"Lord Radal has the right to have a man nearby," Paren assured him. "Now hush during the blessing."

The priest spoke a few words, making the sign of the arrow over them, and they began their slow descent to the temple.

~ ~ ~

Guesare was always an observant man and today he was particularly attentive. Yet he could not find the two faces for which he searched. No doubt, he told himself, they rode down earlier rather than join the procession.

Ahead of him, he could see young Donzalo, leaning to whisper to Radal's aide. The Sharshite was nearly a head shorter than the two Laman men; he seemed a gray mouse beside his brightly clad companions. The minstrel knew this to be illusion. Jobareth was every bit as tall as he, and a well-knit youth, though slender.

Further forward, strode the unmistakable figure of Lord Radal. Guesare was a man of passions. The passion he felt for Radal was hate. He felt it strongly; he felt it more deeply than any hate he had ever known. It was a hate for all that was his opposite, for the cold and cunning soul inhabiting that dark body.

As the procession wound down the hill and out the lowest gate, folk from the countryside began to line the road. These joined them, falling in at the rear. Most were tenant farmers. Serfdom might have disappeared from Lama after the expulsion of the Ani, but the land was still in the hands of the nobles.

Guesare, coming from a society of small freeholders, disapproved. Still, he recognized that different circumstances created different ways. This was a good, rich, peaceful country, unlike his native Cuddon.

Now, the road curved, allowing town and river to be seen. Where Abam joined Weldar stood the largest settlement in Lama, north of Morparas. That great port – a free city, though in the Anian sphere – dwarfed any town of the hinterland.

Through the trees, the minstrel caught a glimpse of the temple roof. They were nearly there.

~ ~ ~

"Your master wore black," whispered Donzalo. "We thought he would."

"The Lord Radal is very careful to maintain the image he has created. For the same reason, I think, he chose not to use a litter." A certain admiration colored the Sharshite's speech. "He pushes himself harder than men half his age."

Donzalo seemed disappointed. "Then the black is but for effect? He doesn't truly prefer it?"

"All he does is well calculated. Radal would have gone naked today, if he thought it to his advantage."

"You are a perceptive fellow, Lector Nafal. The envoy is fortunate to have you."

"That, too, is calculated, I am sure. But," Jobareth laughed, "I have not yet figured it out."

As they went along, the Laman pointed out such local points of interest as existed – often apologetically. At last, they stood before the temple.

"I suppose it is not much compared to those in Sharsh," said Donzalo of the modest sandstone stoa.

"You'd better stay here," Paren suggested. "We must take part in the ceremony."

Jobareth remained by the litters, while the family advanced. On the steps waited the hierophant, a small balding man in robes of red and white. The crowd spread to form a rough arc around them, as priest and parents, Lomela carrying the baby, climbed the short stairway.

Turning at the top, the hierophant led them through a brief ritual of question and response. Then, he marked the boy with ash from the sacred flame, touching shoulders and brow.

"Behold," he announced to those gathered, "Ros!"

Bolos held the child up before them. The crowd erupted in cheers; the babe erupted in tears.

Able to relax now, Donzalo took a look around. Soon, he spotted the two men he sought, one with his eye swollen shut.

Guesare had made his way to his side. "I see them, too."

"Perdos and Percos. I suspected as much."

"You know them?"

"Hangers-on of my brother. Could – could he have aught to do with this?" The idea sickened him.

"It seems unlikely. Have you plans for this afternoon?"

"None. The Ladies Lomela and Vibola will be taking the baby home to rest, while my father and brother remain here, receiving townspeople. I thought perhaps to show the Sharshite around."

They strolled to the spot where Jobareth had stationed himself. "We intend to amuse ourselves in town, Lector. Would you care to join us?" invited the minstrel.

"I thank you, sirs, but no. Lord Radal and I return to the castle. His sergeant has brought down horses for us."

"Ah, then we shall see you this evening, no doubt." Guesare spoke lightly, as if amused by some private jest. "We bid you farewell, young sir, and send our greetings to your master."

6

"If we come upon your attackers, pay them no heed."

"I am not completely witless, Cousin," came Donzalo's good-natured reply.

"No, you are not. Some, I think, judge you too lightly. That," the minstrel emphasized, "is to your advantage."

"You have a plan?"

"We wait for tonight's feast. I want witnesses." Guesare almost slipped on a patch of clay. "Damn this mud." He wiped a spatter from his boldly patterned kilt.

Spring rains had saturated the ground, turning the roadway to mire. Many of those who had gathered at the temple now followed it into town.

"They wouldn't pick a quarrel with us here, would they? Even they should have learned their lesson last night."

"I take it you do not think much of their abilities. Keep in mind," Guesare pointed out, "they almost ended your life."

Sheepishly, the young man agreed and changed the subject. "How does our little county compare to the rest of the world?"

"Why Master Donzalo, to a yokel from the Cuddon, County Rosam is quite impressive, and your town far exceeds anything we have at home."

The Laman persisted. "Your travels are legendary. Tell me of Morparas."

"Many of your friends visit there."

"Yes, but they see it through merchants' eyes, not a poet's."

"Morparas. Big, yes, and dirty, and an evil odor arises from the bay. In many ways, it is but a larger version of this town. It has the same temporary look about it, like the inhabitants might tear it all down one day and start over."

"Have you seen the university?"

"I even sat through some lectures, seeking to improve my Muram."

"I had hoped to study there." Donzalo paused in thought a moment, then decided, "I still do."

"There are better schools in the Siphic cities, or even Sharsh. But," the bard declared, "the great university at Lanlaz is superior to them all."

"In Lorj? You've been to Lorj?" The name of that exotic island evoked wonder – it lay not so distant yet it seemed to be on the other side of the world.

"I have. A pleasant land, though uncomfortably hot. One should visit only during the winter." They had stopped before an inn. "What say you to some ale?"

~ ~ ~

"What *is* he talking about?"

The Lady Lomela looked up from her reading. "I warned you, Grandmother. That sort of thing is stylish in Sharsh, these days. At least," she asserted, smiling, "among young men with too much education."

"Humph. Then I'm glad Donzalo was not allowed to study abroad."

"Your grandson has more interest in cannons than cantos. He might learn many things of value – to him and to his family."

"I suppose it would do the boy good to get out of this backwater for a while." Vibola gave the girl a knowing look. "But we'd both miss him, eh?"

"Yes, Grandmother." Lomela lowered her head again. "Let me find something more interesting." She leafed through the pages. "Here. This one even rhymes."

"Praise be to Kamat."

"It's titled 'In Love's Service,'" she announced gravely, and began to read.

Though oft I wear Love's livery,
No mistress of mine shall she be.
Of Love's bonds I will be free
To sup on life and have my fill,
To take my pleasures where I will;
I'll remain my own man still.

The Lady Vibola sniffed, but said nothing.

So if Love's praises I may sing,
Know that my words mean not a thing;
They are birds that take to wing.
They bear sweet songs to whom they might,
And, leaving naught to mark their flight,
Are away and out of sight.

"He fancies himself quite the gallant."

"I would not take his words too seriously, Grandmother. They are but poetic conceit. There's more."

I'll stay not long in Love's service,
Only a while, to have her kiss.
Then I'll go, rememb'ring this:
She welcomes back all former men,
However long it may have been,
Come to share her gifts again.

She gently shut the book of poems, saying, "That last part, I think, seems forced."

"How like a man," harrumphed the old woman, "to tell himself his infidelity bears no cost."

"My lady, you are much too cynical. Jobareth is not at all that way, really."

"Ah, but he'd like to be."

Lomela broke into gay laughter. "Perhaps we all would, Grandmother." The expression on her oval face then grew quite serious. "Are men truly so fickle?"

"Of course not, girl. I once met one I suspected of being faithful," chuckled Lady Vibola. "No, some men can be true – my Paren, for example. I never understood why he loved Thara, but he did and does still. Even after their son died, he would not hear of divorcing her and taking a younger wife. He said he would rather have Thara than an heir."

"You are not always kind to the Lady Thara." Lomela was a king's daughter and not afraid to express herself.

"I try to be, my dear, but there's a willful old woman in me who sometimes won't behave." She did not sound overly repentant. "That's enough of your friend's poetry; read to me from the *Tales of Borm* a while, will you?"

~ ~ ~

The town had no name; it was simply the town. Travelers might refer to it as Ros-town, particularly those who hailed from one of the other, smaller towns along the Weldar. For most, though, "the town" sufficed.

It was built of wood, this town. Wood was abundant; wood was cheap. Wood did not offend suspicious noblemen.

Donzalo and Guesare ambled down one of the winding, muddy streets. It would lead them, in time, to the river. They had no business at the river, but it was as good a destination as any.

"It takes a good deal of ale to fill you up," commented the Cuddonian.

"I am a larger than normal container," responded his young companion.

"That you are. You could be a formidable fighting man," Guesare told him, "if you wished."

"I do not wish. I am a scholar."

"You may find you have no choice."

Donzalo sighed and walked on a way. "I've been hearing this all my life. 'Remember your birth,' people tell me. 'Think of your duty.'"

"It is the way to which you were born."

"It is a dying way. Power is passing out of our hands, sir, and into those of merchants and tradesmen."

The minstrel considered this novel concept. "As in the Siphic League?"

"Or Sharsh. There the old aristocracy is being squeezed out by the king on one side and the newly wealthy on the other."

"There may be something to that. Such ideas would not endear you to your family."

"I have learned not to speak of them. My father expects me to settle into the life of a landed gentleman, like Uncle Paren. And Bolos thinks I belong in a religious order. However," Donzalo chuckled, "I am not prepared for celibacy."

"That does not seem to bother many priests but I see you would take such vows seriously," observed Guesare. "Even so, religion upholds tradition. You would not fit in there."

"What of you, kinsman? How came you to your calling?"

"There is little choice for a younger son in the Cuddon. Many become mercenaries; I became a minstrel." He added, in explanation, "I do not take discipline well."

"The river is still high." They had reached the banks of the Weldar. "A fortnight ago, we would have been standing knee-deep here."

"It is a mighty flood. Only the Siph is greater."

"Even a small stream might carry one elsewhere," mused Donzalo. "But now, our legs should carry us back to the castle."

"Yes, and we'd best attach ourselves to a group. It would not be wise to be on the road alone."

~ ~ ~

"My lord?"

"What is it, Nafal?"

"May I ask, sir, how much longer we remain here?"

"Through the morrow, at least. Hand me my sash, will you? No, the one with the purple embroidery." Radal tied it about his lean waist. "What thought you of today's ceremony?"

"Terribly boring, sir. These Lamans know nothing of theater."

"They scorn pageantry. You walked beside young Donzalo."

"Yes, my lord."

"Tell me of your conversation."

"It rambled to many subjects. Uh, including you, sir."

"That, I expect."

Indeed, thought Jobareth. Here was a man who did understand theater.

"The Laman told me much of this land. He was also rather interested in my experiences at the university. His desire to go abroad is considerable." The young man hesitated before daring to make a suggestion. "Perhaps, sir, it would be advantageous to have him study in Sharsh."

"Perhaps."

Seeing that Radal had no further comment, he went on "Also, my lord, we spoke of the Lady Lomela. I think he has great affection for her."

"As do you."

The aide swallowed. "As do I, my lord."

"The lady has a talent for attracting loyalty." For once, the Sharshite's smile seemed genuine. "Not unlike her father."

Jobareth knew when to remain silent. Lord Radal's unwavering allegiance to the king was renowned, as was the tale behind it.

"You'd better dress, Nafal. I expect you at the feast, tonight. Make sure the naming gifts are at hand and then feel free to enjoy yourself."

7

Bolos, when he chose, could display the courtly manners expected of him. Even when he drank too much – which was often – the ingrained habits of a noble upbringing carried him through.

Borrago's heir was neither a particularly good nor a particularly bad man, just as he was neither particularly tall nor short, clever nor dull. He was an ordinary sort of fellow who found it all too easy to indulge his appetites. It told in his thick waist and red face, in his blurred and blood-shot eyes. Already, he was into his cups.

Jobareth Nafal greeted his master at the door of the great hall.

"Yon lordling will drink himself to an early death," Lord Radal whispered to his aide. "We must be prepared when it comes."

"Yes, my lord. Sir Paren asks when we wish to present. Sharsh can be first, if you desire, or just before the final gift. That would be the Count Borrago's."

"What do you think?"

Jobareth had already considered this problem. "First, sir. We need not invite comparisons with the count."

"Let it be so." The envoy was approving. "You have the makings of a true diplomat."

"Thank you, my lord. Your seat is at the high table."

"Of course."

"Yes, of course, sir. No one is being announced but there should be an attendant around. Here he is now, my lord." A servitor had approached them. "You will show the ambassador to his place?"

"This way, my lord," said the man. With a Laman's typical disregard for ceremony, he started away.

"Hold a moment," requested Radal. In a low voice, he asked Jobareth "Where will you be?"

"Some of Lady Lomela's friends asked me to sit with them, sir. That will be on your – left, about half-way down the hall."

"Try to keep an eye on the Cuddonian minstrel. Don't worry if you can't; it's not overly important. Report to me in the morning." He turned to the attendant. "Lead on."

~ ~ ~

Tonight, little Ros had the place of honor, propped up in an ornately carved crib for all to see. To his right sat his father and, beyond him, Borrago. His mother was to the left and to her left, Lord Radal, as representative of her father.

Bolos made a short speech welcoming the guests. He was not yet too far gone for that. Soon he would be, now that his duty was done.

So was the baby's. He had made his appearance and, after a few minutes, his nurse carried him away.

Radal felt a hand upon his left arm.

"Is not that tunic terribly uncomfortable, my lord?"

His garment was long, heavy, and stiff with embroidery. It might be normal wear for formal occasions in Sharsh, but he saw that most of the other guests wore knee-length tunics, or kilts in the Cuddonian style.

"Indeed it is, Countess Vibola."

The old woman's smile was radiant. "Hardly anyone remembers that is still my title." She tipped her head "So why wear it?"

"It is what a well-dressed gentleman of Sharsh dons for such an affair." He shrugged in mock resignation. "I have no choice, my lady."

"My husband never wore such a get-up, and he was as fine a gentleman of Sharsh as any."

He found this elderly noblewoman's bluntness somewhat disconcerting. "Both times and fashions change, madame."

"But not for the better."

"Lady Vibola, are you pestering the ambassador?" chided a voice at his other elbow.

"My lady," protested the Sharshite lord, "it is a pleasure to converse with two such fascinating and lovely companions."

The women exchanged incredulous looks.

"I have known Lord Radal all my life. Don't be taken in by his smooth manner," warned Lomela. "His daughter was my playmate. How fares the Lady Fachalana, sir?"

"As rebellious and troublesome as ever, I fear. She refuses every suitor, my lady, and fancies herself an actress."

"Does she wear black, too?" inquired Vibola, all pretend innocence.

Lady Lomela choked back her laughter. "Hush. There is an entertainment."

It was the first of several. Acrobats, musicians, even an itinerant company of players had found their way to Castle Rosam. One of the resident bards presented a preposterous poem in honor of the occasion. The other, not to be outdone, droned through an interminable saga of the first Ros.

Lady Lomela leaned forward to address Vibola. "Why isn't Sir Guesare performing this evening, my lady?"

"He excused himself, claiming some pressing, private need."

Donzalo, seated beyond his grandmother, kept his eyes on Lord Radal, but the envoy betrayed neither interest nor emotion. He noted the boy, however, and smiled inwardly.

~ ~ ~

"This is going on forever. When will the gifting begin?"

"Next," Paren told his brother. "I sent the word to your steward."

Thanks to his loud voice, Saj, Master of Hounds, at times served also as herald. Now, he announced the origin of each gift and servants brought it forth.

Sharsh's presents, though showy, seemed small; they had been carried swiftly, and from a distance, on horseback. A richly worked golden cup and an ornate pistol were displayed.

"The gunne is made in Sharsh," whispered Paren. "Pretty, but not to be compared with those from the Siphics."

Borrago nodded his agreement. "Have you seen that pair Guesare carries?"

A procession of lesser offerings followed, the gifts of Laman noblemen; the wealthy commoners had been received earlier in the day. Presents ranged from weapons to furniture to jewelry and even a puppy.

"Every boy needs a dog," announced its somewhat tipsy donor.

"Wake up, Bolos." The count nudged his son. "My gift is coming."

A handsome saddle, suited to a pony, came forth, and a skillfully painted wooden horse, as well.

"Until the boy's old enough to ride," the proud grandfather informed his heir, but Bolos had again dozed off.

"I'll give the thank you speech," sighed Borrago.

~ ~ ~

Radal's aide had quickly grown bored. These young nobles were a shallow lot, with their gossip and talk of fashions. He found himself watching Guesare.

The minstrel was seated not far from Jobareth. He, too, seemed to be watching someone. The Sharshite soon recognized that the object of Guesare's interest was the two men he had passed outside his quarters.

Turning to one of his companions, he asked, "Know you those two gentlemen?" He nodded in their direction. "The two big fellows."

The plump young man looked up from his plate. "No gentlemen those," he replied, wiping his fingers fastidiously, "though someone saw fit to confer knighthood on them. They belong to the garrison here – part of Sir Bolos's private guard. Brother Grippo, do you remember yon ruffians' names? Bolos's bullies over there."

"Perdos and Percos," answered his tablemate, who wore the robe of an acolyte. "Scum from the northern marches."

"Yes, of course. Bad sorts. Best stay away from them, Lector."

"Good advice. I thank you, sirs." Nafal sipped his wine. "This is not bad stuff. A local vintage?" The young man knew wines, for his family had made its fortune in their trade.

"Surely it doesn't compare with the wines of Sharsh!" objected the fat Laman.

"Sharsh produces its share of swill, but it doesn't find its way across the mountains to you."

Something was going on. The last gifts had been presented and guests began moving about the hall.

He sipped again. "I'd imagine that your summers are too hot to produce truly great wines. Now in Arolin – " From the corner of his eye, he saw Guesare approach the two knights.

"Ah, you will excuse me, gentlemen. I must attend to some business for my master." He rose abruptly and moved closer to the minstrel.

With easy insolence, the Cuddonian looked Perdos over. "What happened to this pretty face?"

"My brother, uh, fell and hurt himself."

"Brothers, eh? Are you certain you are not half-brothers?"

Percos scratched his head. "What's he mean by that?"

"You fool! He insulted Mother!"

As he grasped the meaning of Guesare's words, Percos reddened. "Hey, you don't even know our mother!"

"I know her reputation. All Lama knows her reputation."

The inebriated knight was not difficult to provoke. "I demand satisfaction!" he bellowed in the bard's smirking face.

"Then meet me on the field of honor."

"Tomorrow!" seethed Percos.

"Nay, the tourney is tomorrow." Master Saj had stepped between them. "If you must duel, let it be the next day."

~ ~ ~

"We know now the nature of Guesare's personal business," stated Lady Vibola.

"But what," asked Lomela, "Could he possibly have to do with those two?"

"He was responsible for Perdos's face," Donzalo informed them. He escorted the two women to his grandmother's rooms. "There was an – incident last night."

"That sounds intriguing. Will you come in and tell us about it?"

"Indeed I will, my lady. The minstrel asked me to remain with you until he arrived."

Donzalo opened the heavy oak door for them and they entered, passing into one of the smaller chambers. There, Lady Vibola's most recent maidservant – none lasted long with her – helped her to her seat by the fire.

"Your ambassador is charming," the old woman observed, settling herself. She smoothed her deep crimson gown and tossed aside the shawl she had worn against the coolness of the evening air.

"He would cut your throat – or mine – in an instant if he felt it in the interests of Sharsh."

"I would never doubt it."

"Yet," Lady Lomela admitted, "he can be charming, though you know it all is but a game with him – and he knows that you know." She turned to Donzalo. "What game does Lord Radal play with you?"

"With me, my lady?"

"I saw you watching him," she accused, "as I saw him carefully ignoring you."

The young man sighed. "You are better schooled in intrigue than I, Lomela."

"What is going on, Donni?" asked his grandmother.

"It seems the Lady Lomela's father wants me dead." Donzalo tried to speak as calmly, as matter-of-factly, as possible, ignoring the fear growing within him. This was more than a game.

Lomela, although surprised, readily accepted his statement. "But why?"

"I know not the whole story." A knocking came at the door. "That will be Guesare; I'll let him tell it."

8

"Was it safe for you to come here by yourself?" Lomela asked, when Guesare finished his tale.

"They would not dare attack me after our public quarrel. That's one reason I provoked it."

"The Lord Radal might," she warned. "He would care little if suspicion fell on two such minions."

"True, but he will wait a while, I think, before risking direct action." The Cuddonian turned to Donzalo. "Young sir, will you serve as my squire tomorrow?"

"Me, Guesare?" came the confused reply. "You mean at the tournament?"

"Perdos would like to get a crack at me before I duel his brother. If I enter the joust, he most certainly will as well, in hopes of doing me harm."

"I'm honored, sir, but I know little of the, uh, knightly arts." He didn't say so, but Donzalo thought the tournament terribly old-fashioned.

"It matters not; I seek chiefly to keep you nearby," explained the minstrel, becoming quite serious. "Henceforth, for your safety, we should remain close."

Lady Vibola spoke up. "Why don't you two stay here tonight? I have far more room than I need. But don't," she chuckled, "tell your father that, Donzalo."

"Should we tell him any of the rest of this?" wondered the young man.

"In time," Guesare answered. "No point in doing so, now."

"Yes," agreed Lomela. "He'd probably go straight to Radal in his anger."

"And we have no solid proof," the minstrel pointed out. "There is naught more to be done." He reached for his rebec. "How about a song?"

~ ~ ~

"I like this little hill." The ambassador pointed toward a grassy piece of land beside the road. "What think you of it as the site of our embassy?"

"It seems an excellent location." Radal must have made note of it the previous day. "We would have one built, sir?"

"Eventually, and it would be your job to see it done. At first, though, you'll need to find lodging in the town."

"Not in the castle, my lord?"

"No. We are a powerful and independent nation, not just another little county or city-state. The Lamans must be reminded of that fact."

"Yes, certainly, sir," Jobareth answered, and then made bold to add, "and it gives us a certain privacy."

Lord Radal nodded. "Indeed. I expect you to make as many contacts in the town as in the castle. Anyone," he emphasized, "no matter how mean, can prove useful."

The Sharshites accompanied a party riding down from Castle Rosam. "This is a different road," observed the ambassador, as they turned to the right.

"It takes us around the town, my lord. The tourney is to the north." The aide shaded his eyes. "I can see the pennants and tents of the fair from here."

"I fear this day will be wasted," sighed Radal, "but we depart in the morning. Be certain all is ready."

"Yes, my lord." So they would not stay for the duel. Jobareth thought that odd, as his master had shown considerable interest in the situation. "Will it be early, sir?"

"I hope so. If I finish our business with the count today, we can leave well before the dawn."

~ ~ ~

A level field beside the Weldar had long served as Borrago's fair ground. In the summer, it found constant use; this was a center of trade for all of Lama. But such crowds as gathered now were unusual so early in the year.

Even the well-traveled Cuddonian was impressed.

"You should be here at mid-summer," Donzalo told him. "It's said to be the largest fair in the world."

"The world is very wide. Yet, I admit I have never seen larger." Guesare gazed across a sea of tents and booths. "The taxes must overflow your father's coffers."

"There is an income from rents and river tolls, and more to be made, indirectly, by the fostering of trade in our lands. It has been my dream to establish greater manufacture here." There was passion in the young man's voice. "We depend too much on imports."

They had come to an open space, with box seats along one side. "Now this must be the site of our tourney."

"Do you intend to joust on that horse?" Guesare straddled his rugged pony of the Cuddon.

"Nay. I have been lent a charger by one of my kinsmen." The minstrel laughed. "He hopes to fill his pockets wagering on me."

The river edged the field to the west and the seating spread along the other side. Pavilions stood at either end, for the use of the contestants.

"No one in the boxes yet," noted Donzalo. "Not many spectators at all."

"'Tis early. Let's find the heralds and get ourselves sorted out."

~ ~ ~

A succession of diversions filled the morning: shooting competitions with both bow and gunne, races, displays of horsemanship, even wrestling matches. The knightly events would be held in the afternoon.

Radal found himself bored. The count would not grant him the few minutes needed for a serious discussion, and only one contest held interest for the noble of Sharsh. He waited impatiently for the jousting.

Briefly, Lord Radal had considered risking magic last night. Better, he decided, to wait; the truly effective spells required time and concentration. If Perdos failed against the Cuddonian, he would call upon his powers tonight. If Guesare fell, leaving young Donzalo unprotected, more ordinary agents might be employed.

Borrago, notoriously tight with his money, provided no lunch. It was necessary to send young Jobareth among the vendors. He returned with meat – pork, they assumed – smothered in spicy sauce, and a sort of fried cake popular in Lama. Both Sharshites found the fare indigestible.

Then began the joust. Full armor was a rarity here, and specialized tilting armor, unknown. The combatants wore what plate or mail they possessed, and wrapped themselves and their steeds in heavy quilting. With blunt lances, that usually sufficed.

"Sit beside me, Nafal," requested the envoy. "Put away your tablet; no more dictation today." Radal had kept them both busy all morning with the reading and answering of dispatches.

The aide took a seat by his master.

"Do you follow the joust, boy?"

"Not really, my lord. It seems dated."

"I suppose it is. Still, a lancer can be a deadly fighting man."

"No doubt, sir, but I would not care to charge massed musketry."

"In this part of the world, the gunne is less of a factor in war."

The younger man nodded. That will change, he thought to himself.

Aloud, he commented, "You are well known as an enthusiast, my lord."

"Ah, a shift in focus, and very tactfully done, too," approved Lord Radal. "I was never much in the lists, myself, but I squired for King Lareth when I was young – Prince Lareth, then."

Jobareth knew this story: a youthful Radal, snubbed by the old aristocracy of Sharsh, had become Lareth's protege. The two's destinies had been intertwined almost from the start.

"Despite the crudities of this tournament, we may see some very good performances today." The ambassador's interest seemed genuine. "They take their tilting seriously here in Lama."

9

"Our Sharshites finally seem to be paying attention."

"Lord Radal is a great patron of the tourney," Lomela told her husband. "Have you any favorites?"

"My man Perdos is handy with the lance."

"Sir Guesare is said to be quite skillful, as well. I think it likely they will meet before the day is done."

Bolos scowled. "I hope Perdos unhorses that Eastern show-off."

"He probably hopes to do more than just unhorse the man."

"Oh, yes, the duel." He frowned at his wife. "My brother talks to you. Why would he choose to squire for the Cuddonian? Is it to spite me?"

"They have become friends. That's all, I'm sure."

"I know what sort of friendship this Guesare prefers. I have long suspected Donzalo of being the same."

Lomela smiled at the absurdity of his idea. "I think not, Bolos, I think not."

The first two entrants stood ready at either end of the field. These Lamans might not have had the steeds and armor of noble Western jousters, but they knew their business well. As they hurtled forward, paths separated by a low fence, their lances were aimed squarely at each other's shield.

"A clean strike," Lomela commented.

"And neither unhorsed." Bolos sounded disappointed. "Some wine, my lady?" he queried, filling his goblet from a jug. "Damn, I'm out."

"That's all right, my lord husband. Perhaps later."

Bolos motioned to an attendant as the jousters prepared for another pass. This time, one went down into the mud.

~ ~ ~

"All you need do is stand here with a spare lance. Hand me up my shield now, will you?" requested Guesare. "And move those steps out of the way." The knight had used them to mount his tall charger.

"Here you go, sir. Good luck!" Donzalo watched the dashing

Cuddonian gallop onto the field and rein his tall, dappled steed in dramatically. Guesare knew how to play to a crowd. Then, becoming serious, the knight turned to the work at hand. He quickly disposed of his opponent, knocking him from the saddle in one pass, and returned to his novice squire. Donzalo took shield and lance, brought the wooden steps, and helped him dismount.

"Too easy," Guesare remarked.

"You should meet Perdos in the fourth round," the young Laman told him. "If you both make it that far," he added.

"Barring bad luck, we shall. The man showed ability in his first match. What he lacks in technique, he makes up in strength."

Twice more, both knights readily unhorsed those they met. Only four contestants remained.

Donzalo expressed his concerns. "The scoundrel will not fight cleanly, I fear."

"Nor shall I," came the Easterner's retort. "But neither of us will be so blatant as to commit a foul. At least, not right away."

The other pair was to go first. Donzalo pointed out one knight, well-mounted, well-armored.

"That is Sorsen, son of Count Orgelo. He has quite a reputation as a fighter."

"I know of him, and of the count. Both staunchly anti-Sharsh."

"Their borders lie too close to the mountains."

Guesare nodded. "What of this other lad? One of your father's men, isn't he?"

"Copago, his master of arms – and my half-brother, by rumor."

"Indeed?" The minstrel raised his eyebrows. "That is one I had not heard."

"My father was discreet. Sir Copago dearly dislikes Perdos and would welcome the chance to face him."

"I shall do my best to disappoint the fellow. If not," he laughed, "perhaps I can soften up his opponent for him."

"Do not count Sorsen out. He is certainly the better equipped."

"But less skilled at tilting. His experience has been in more practical forms of combat."

Sir Sorsen was impressive. He could not match the flamboyance of Guesare but, rather, his appearance tended toward the imposing. The tall nobleman wore a closed helm, black, as was his armor. Black, too, was the fiery steed he straddled. Both were bedecked in his colors of blue and white.

At the other end of the field waited Copago. The man was short and muscular, more resembling Count Borrago than either of his legitimate heirs. Though not as well accoutered as his foe, Copago's position had enabled him to find adequate, if mismatched, armor, as well as his choice of the count's warhorses.

The herald – not Master Saj, but a professional of the tournaments, resplendent in dark blue cloak and turban – gave the signal to charge. In one pass it was over. Sorsen lay flat on his back.

~ ~ ~

"Perfectly struck!" exclaimed Lord Radal.

"Is the – yes, Sir Sorsen is rising. The crowd cheers him, my lord."

"He seems unhurt." The ambassador had a sour look about him; he did not share the people's affection for Sorsen. "I would not mind seeing harm come to Orgelo's boy," he admitted, "but not in the tourney, of course."

Jobareth had doubts as to his master's sincerity. Radal, he suspected, was trying to maintain his image as an even-handed patron of the tournament.

Sorsen saluted the crowd, and gave a short bow to his vanquisher before leaving the field.

"I know Count Orgelo leads the opposition to Sharsh," said the aide. "Do you consider him that much of a threat, sir?"

"Yes, but let us not discuss politics now. I have particular interest in the next match-up."

Jobareth looked to the neighboring box and chuckled. "My lord, the Lady Lomela attempts to waken her husband. They must have concerns of their own about its outcome."

"Backing opposite sides, I imagine," mused the envoy. "As are we? What say you to a wager, young sir?"

"I say only a fool wagers with his master, my lord."

"We wager every time we speak, Nafal. You have played the game well, so far."

True enough, thought the young Sharshite. But where he risked his career, Radal gambled for larger stakes. "Thank you, sir," he replied, suddenly leery of saying too much.

The older man smiled with what seemed to be true warmth. "Remember, my boy, it is but a game. Now, do you think this Cuddonian popinjay truly has a chance?"

"There is more to him, my lord, than his manner would suggest. We have seen that on the field today."

"He depends over much on natural talent. The Laman may not possess the most polished of technique, but he is a solid performer."

"Yes, sir, he seems a hard man to unhorse."

"Exactly. If each strikes dead-center on his opponent's shield, Sir Perdos should have the better of it."

"But Guesare will avoid that, won't he, my lord?" asked Jobareth. He had but the sketchiest understanding of jousting strategy.

"He will try. It's a classic contest: finesse versus strength."

The two adversaries moved into position. Neither seemed to hold an advantage in armor or mount. At a sign from the herald, they hurtled toward each other.

10

Copago knew he was not well liked. His manner could be brusque, even harsh. He was too demanding for some. Others resented what they saw as favoritism shown to him by the count. But Copago knew also he had earned what he had achieved and that he demanded more from himself than anyone else. As for his manner, that couldn't be helped; it was who he was.

He stood now, watching the contest between Guesare and Perdos. His brother, acting as his squire, stood beside him. Both knew they were half-brothers. Neither had ever mentioned it.

"These two want to hurt each other," commented the younger man.

"There seems to be enmity between them. You know of the duel?"

"Indeed, yes. I was there when the Cuddonian provoked it. Oddly enough," he continued, "the young Sharshite aide seemed to be expecting something of the sort."

"It's politics, then." The master of arms spat the words out. "You are fortunate, Grippo, to be entering the priesthood, beyond all this."

"And you are naive, brother, to think there is no intrigue in the temple. They're set for a second run."

"Let's see if Guesare aims high on the shield again."

"He hopes to wear down his opponent? Render his shield arm useless?"

"Or, at least, tire it. It's a risky tactic; he must avoid the brunt of Perdos's attack."

The combatants came together. For the second time, Guesare managed to send his enemy's weapon glancing away with minimal impact. His own strike, again high, caused the Laman's buckler to fly upward. Its edge caught Perdos in the face, opening a cut above his eye.

Copago whistled. "That was pretty."

"I trust you are not referring to the Northerner's face," joked his brother. Grippo was as light-hearted as his sibling was sober.

The knight gave him a smile, but quickly became serious once more. "Whichever of these two succeeds," he stated, "may be in no shape to face me."

~~~

As Donzalo moved forward to tend Guesare, the herald approached them, his expression stern.

"I warn you, sir, we will tolerate no deliberate attempts to injure your adversary."

The knight nodded. "Certainly, Herald." He threw his spear to the ground. "Donzalo, my lance has split. Hand me up a new one."

The man rode to Perdos to issue the same message.

"This time," Guesare confided, "I aim low."

Donzalo's look expressed his confusion. What was the Cuddonian attempting?

"He thinks my tactic is to attack his arm. I look to catch him off-balance."

Once more, the two thundered toward each other. This time, Guesare did catch his opponent off-balance. But Perdos caught him squarely, as well, and both men went to the ground.

A crew of attendants immediately filled the field, catching the horses, picking up the shattered lances, and helping the jousters to their feet. Donzalo remained at his post, for that was the custom, and waited anxiously.

Neither was incapacitated; there would be another round.

"Perdos must be growing frustrated. I expect him to disregard the rules on this pass," said Guesare. "There's the herald; time to mount up."

Donzalo understood. These men were not concerned with winning. They wished only to hurt each other. He helped the minstrel up the steps and onto his steed; he could feel that the man was starting to stiffen up.

"I shall try to finish him," Guesare continued, from the saddle. "This may be my best opportunity."
~~~

~ ~ ~

"Why doesn't that idiot finish him?" grumbled Bolos.

"We shall see a winner this time, I feel certain," Lady Lomela told him, "or else a disqualification."

"Oh?" Her husband turned to her in interest. "You anticipate a foul?"

"By one or both," she replied. "They are beyond caring."

"I must have you along the next time I lay a bet," Bolos declared, half-serious, half-mocking. "I did not realize that you were so knowledgeable."

"There is much, my lord husband, that you do not know about me."

For a moment, he sat in silence. "Yes, I have neglected you." He looked again at his wife. "You think me a drunken clod."

"You think yourself one, Bolos," she answered, "and you must decide whether you are."

Bolos said nothing. Lomela was uncertain whether the man pondered her words or was merely confused by them. At last, she chose to break the awkward silence.

"They stand ready."

"Yes." The nobleman unsteadily poured another goblet of wine, red drops splattering his already stained tunic. "Now we shall see."

Again, the jousters rushed forward. Their lances were held steady, though Perdos's shield drooped noticeably. Suddenly, his point went low – low enough to be considered a foul. It seemed that he meant to slip under his opponent's shield in hopes of striking hip or leg, or, failing that, horse.

But Guesare was still too quick, too agile. He maneuvered shield and steed sufficiently to catch the tip and send it sliding harmlessly away. His own lance impacted the top of Perdos's sagging shield, then smashed into his shoulder.

Perdos fell; the Cuddonian rode on to the cheers of the crowd.

Bolos regarded his wife with new admiration. "You guessed right, my lady."

"Everyone knew the two disliked each other," she replied modestly. They watched Perdos struggle to his feet, his left arm hanging limp. "I think your man is hurt."

"Might be a broken arm."

"Or collar bone."

"Either way," concluded Bolos, "he'll find it hard to second his brother tomorrow."

~ ~ ~

"If the Easterner has any sense, he will forfeit the final match."

"Yes, my lord," agreed Jobareth. "He has accomplished what he intended."

"Exactly. And he has the morrow to consider." Not that I will permit him to reach his duel, Radal told himself. The man must be dealt with tonight – and the boy, as well.

On the field, preparations had been made for the last match. The master of arms now waited, his fiery charger stamping impatiently. A few moments later, Guesare mounted up and rode forward to deafening applause.

Radal laughed scornfully. "He needs play to the rabble. The man is a fool."

Or wishes us to think he is, thought the aide. There was plotting here, he knew, to which he was not privy.

The crowd cheered wildly as the tilters came together to touch lances in a gesture of respect, then galloped back to their posts. There, they whirled to face each other, and, at the herald's mark, charged.

Despite the lack of armor and fine horses, despite the lack of pomp and show, all knew that these two were the equals of any jouster out of Sharsh, and that this contest was very much as exciting as any held before the court of King Lareth. Lances level, shields steady, they crashed into their opponents.

Both men reeled, but neither fell.

As they returned to their starting points, however, Guesare slumped in the saddle. The herald immediately rode to him. After conferring briefly, he went to the center of the field and signaled that Copago was the winner.

"He cannot continue!" exclaimed Radal. "He has forfeited."

"Do you think it a serious injury, my lord?" inquired Jobareth.

The ambassador shrugged. "Let us pray it is not." He mouthed the words, but obviously did not mean them. Why, his aide wondered, was Radal not bothering to conceal his feelings?

"Ah, the count is motioning to me. At last, I can conclude my business with him."

11

Donzalo was concerned. "Should I fetch a doctor?"

"No, lad," whispered Guesare, leaning on his friend's arm. "I am uninjured. This is all for show." Grimacing, he gripped his midsection. "Let them believe I've cracked a few ribs."

"You feigned your hurt?" The young man's eyes traveled to Sir Copago, receiving the accolades of the crowd.

"There seemed no need to take on yon champion again. Honor was served and chances are he would have unhorsed me, anyway," he informed his companion. "Why risk harm with tomorrow's doings hanging over us?"

"But you felt it worthwhile to take one pass?" wondered Donzalo. "Just so our enemies would think you injured?"

"And also think me foolhardy. Which, perhaps, I am. I could not bear to withdraw without making at least one run at the fellow." Guesare regarded his erstwhile opponent with unconcealed admiration. "He is very good, you know. Is he a friend?"

"He is no enemy. His devotion to duty leaves him room for few friends, but we do share, um, certain interests."

An attendant approached them. "Shall I send for a litter, Master Donzalo?"

"Yes, thank you. We wish to depart for the castle at once."

Guesare watched the man hurry away. "All the servants seem to like you," he mused. "That's a good sign. Shared interests, you say?"

"In armaments, fortifications, that sort of thing. He helped me get that old trebuchet into operation."

"A useful man to have on your side, Donzalo."

"I have a side?"

~ ~ ~

"So the ambassador's taking his leave of us?"

"Yes. He plans to depart tonight."

"None too soon for me, Borri."

The count nodded his agreement. "When will you be going?"

"There is no great hurry," Paren told him, "though I miss the peace of my home."

"Peace on the edge of the Cuddon? Those hills team with wild men and wild beasts," protested Borrago, "and other beings, more dangerous."

"Oh, those don't bother us. The occasional troll wanders down, but they're not much trouble. Some are downright friendly."

The two rode on without speaking. Their entourage followed at a discreet distance.

After a time, Paren brought up a subject that had been on his mind. "Have you thought on my offer yet? Will you let Donzalo come home with us?"

"If he's willing, I am. Did you speak to him?"

"I wanted to hear from you first."

"He may be less than enthusiastic," warned Borrago. "The boy has never shown any interest in farming."

"Let's call it a short visit, a month or two, and see if it can be stretched into autumn," his brother suggested. "Once he gets there, he may find much to divert him."

"He'll probably want to rebuild your walls," chuckled the count, "or dam up the Abam."

"I've been considering doing that. He gave me the idea last year."

"Would it work?"

"I think so. If nothing else, I'd have a place to go fishing. That project would keep him happy for a while."

"It might be just the lure to get him there," Borrago felt. "I trust you will do your best to school him in running a manor."

"And in the obligations of his station. With luck, he'll be ready for knighthood when he returns."

"Donzalo needs to get away from the influences of this place. I don't like him spending all his time with merchants and minstrels." The count looked up. "Here's the last gate. Let's talk further tonight."

~ ~ ~

The way from the Sharshites' quarters to those of Lady Lomela was not long. Long enough, though, for Jobareth to have time to think. Now he hesitated outside her door.

Why had she invited him here to a private dinner? Was it only to say farewell or something more? Such questions might not have occurred to him two days earlier.

And what was his master's purpose? He had locked himself in his room with orders that he remain undisturbed. Radal's grim look had told his aide that he did not seek rest.

Jobareth knew that this mission involved more than simply presenting gifts or studying the diplomatic situation. There was plotting here he could not hope to comprehend.

He rapped lightly on the door. It was a plain affair, unadorned pine, as was much of this place. A plump middle-aged woman opened to him.

"Why, Mistress Traspa," said he in surprise. "I did not know you were in Lama."

"Someone has to care for my lady among these savages," replied the dowdy maid. "Come on in, boy."

For a moment, Jobareth considered telling her it was "Lector," but he realized Lomela's loyal servant would always think of him as a boy. She had known him too long.

"Will, uh, anyone else be joining us?" he asked her. A note of anxiety had slipped into his voice; too much was going on.

The maid thought she understood his nervousness. "You mean the husband? I can count the nights he has spent in my lady's rooms on one hand. And, then," she confided, "He mostly was too drunk to do more than pass out."

"But surely he visits? Takes meals with her?"

Traspa shook her head. "Not Bolos. I guess he sees all he wants of her and she doesn't complain about his lack of attention. Give me your cloak, young master, and I'll tell the lady you're here."

He handed the garment to her. "Doesn't anyone come here?"

"Our Lomela does most of her socializing elsewhere. A few lady friends call. And Donzalo – the count's younger son."

"I know him."

She nodded. "He drops by frequently. In fact, he and that minstrel were here earlier." The maid went into the next room.

Lomela occupied a small suite, a floor above the great hall. Though not as spacious as Lady Vibola's quarters, the rooms were lighter and less stuffy, being on a corner. It was certainly an improvement over the windowless dungeon assigned to the visitors from Sharsh.

"The baby will stay in his nurse's room all night, my lady," Traspa was telling the princess as they entered. "Shall I attend you?" She suspected that her mistress would desire privacy.

"No, thank you. Someone will be coming up from the kitchen. Why don't you go down there and find that cook you're forever making eyes at?"

"My lady! I merely admire his culinary skills," objected a blushing Traspa. "Though any man who can prepare such delightful desserts will find a soft spot in my heart." Having hurriedly wrapped herself in a shawl, she paused at the door to promise, "I'll tell them to send your meal up at once."

"Come with me, Jobareth," requested Lomela. "Did you know this is the only room in the castle with a balcony? Not," she added, "that there's anything worth seeing from it." They stepped out onto a small platform overlooking the main gate.

"Lady Vibola and her count occupied these rooms. He added this whole wing when they married. I wonder how many times she saw him pass through that gate." She sighed. "And one time, he didn't return. The lady continued to live here until Borrago's wife died."

"You seem in a somber mood, my lady."

"Yes." Lomela brightened, yet seemed wistful still. "It must be this balcony. But I can speak to you out here with assurance of not being overheard."

Then, another change of mood: the young woman became serious. "Sir Guesare was not sure I should trust you. You are my friend?" She raised her questioning green eyes to his.

"Always, my lady."

"I need a friend. Listen well, Jobareth, and do not disappoint me."

12

This was a risk, Radal knew. There would be suspicion; indeed, many would feel certain that his hand was involved. So be it.

There had been one bit of fortune. Guesare had chosen to spend the night in Donzalo's quarters. The minstrel would seem the target of this attack and the boy no more than an unfortunate bystander. Suspicion might even be directed toward Perdos and Percos.

In any event, best he be gone before the deed was discovered. Spies enough remained behind to keep him informed, Traspa not the least of them. It was Lomela's maid who had told him of Donzalo's whereabouts and had brought hairs from the boy's head, essential for this spell. He had done well to recruit her, before ever she left Sharsh – all the more since Traspa believed she served the interests of her mistress.

Such magics as he would raise tonight were no slight undertaking. They would require all his strength and all his concentration. The guard posted at his door had the strictest of orders; no one would be allowed to interrupt, no matter what the emergency.

The Sharshite opened a small cask, ebony bound with iron, and removed a skull. A grim smile touched his lips as he looked upon all that remained of his instructor in the black arts, a mighty mage in his day. A man into whom he had slipped a knife when the time was right.

Radal raised the relic high. "Asak!" he cried. "Asak! Asak!"

~ ~ ~

Jobareth hurried back to his room, carrying far too many thoughts. At least, he now had a much clearer understanding of his master's motivations. But why, he wondered, was young Donzalo considered a threat? Neither he nor Lomela could find a reason there.

Yet it seemed that she withheld some secret, something she was not ready to share. Having known the princess most of his life, he also knew her moods, her thoughts, her ways.

For Jobareth Nafal loved Lomela. From his first visit to the royal court, he had adored her. He had been five, she, three, and they had grown up together, princess and bookish boy, playing in the gardens of King Lareth. There in the shade of the arbored roses, she had first kissed him. There they had kissed farewell, more than a year ago.

He had reached the envoy's chambers. At the door was posted a guard, as usual. This, however, was not any guard but the sergeant of the small troop that had accompanied them to Lama, Radal's most trusted man-at-arms. Jobareth nodded and hastened by. The fellow always made him uncomfortable. He had heard tales of Sergeant Sojel's habits, his cruelty to both men and women. The soldier ignored him, with an impassiveness almost insolent. Sojel held the young scholar in very low regard and made no attempt to hide it.

As he passed, Nafal could not help but note the cold green lights that flickered from below his master's door. He had never before witnessed Radal's infamous magics but knew instinctively that there were spells being cast behind that locked and guarded slab of oak. He shivered despite himself, aware that Sojel would mark his reactions and sneer, as he continued down the hall.

In his own small room at last, the Sharshite began the sorting through of this evening's events. Of one thing he was certain: he had chosen the side of Lomela – and Donzalo – over that of Radal and the king. It was a dangerous choice. It was the only choice.

"You are a fool," Jobareth Nafal told himself. "You have no business playing such games." Having decided that, he began to prepare for departure. His master wished to take leave of this place in a few hours.

~ ~ ~

Guesare had not been allotted the best of quarters. He had, in fact, been given a bed in the stables, a space shared with sundry other visitors of lesser rank. Now he and his gear were settled in Donzalo's rooms.

"You know, boy," he had confided, "that people will talk. I have a, uh, certain reputation." For once, the minstrel seemed somewhat unsure.

Donzalo found that amusing. He also fleetingly wondered why the man should be concerned about his reputation. "It will only confirm my brother's suspicions. I have no fear of such gossip." He spread his arms. "Make yourself at home. There's not much to the place."

The young noble spoke truthfully. He occupied two small untidy rooms against the west wall, above the barracks. The rear wall of his sleeping chamber was the stone castle wall itself; the rest was built of sturdy oak. This was one of the oldest sections of Keep Rosam, built, in fact, when the place was still in Anian hands.

"I'll spread my blanket here among your books." Guesare gazed admiringly at the collection lining the walls. "You must have the largest library north of Morparas."

His host did not bother to conceal his pride. "I think so. I certainly have more in this room than are found in the entire rest of the castle. Here, look." He pulled down a volume. "This was brought across the Central Sea."

The bard puzzled over the strange script for a moment. "Can you read this?" he asked.

"It seems to be a dialect of Muram. But," continued Donzalo, "it also appears to be the same text as this." A small tattered book was passed to Guesare.

"A treasure!" exclaimed the Cuddonian. He looked up at the lad with narrowed eyes. "Know you what this is?"

"I know it is very ancient. I also know it to be a treatise on magic."

His guest nodded. "Indeed, quite ancient. This particular volume would seem to be from Lorj. No?"

"Yes." Donzalo crouched beside the minstrel and turned pages in the book. "Here," he said, pointing. "Coradean, some six hundred years ago."

"Ah. But this other text is far, far older. Thousands of years, I would think."

"You know of such things?"

"I have a smattering of knowledge. With enemies such as Radal it is needed. Oh," Guesare added, "the white magics only, I assure you."

"The priests assure us that all magic is black."

"Their own rites are white magic by another name. I must study these someday," he remarked, returning the volumes to Donzalo. "Not tonight. I've a duel to fight on the morrow and should rest."

~ ~ ~

Radal was not an old man, but the powerful magics take their toll. He seemed now aged far beyond his years, his face become a skull to match that of his long-dead mentor. Slowly, he replaced that old object of power in its cask, closed the small grimoire he carried ever on his person, and sagged into a chair.

I have done what I can, he told himself. There was no way to tell whether his spells had achieved his desired ends. That news should reach him in Sharsh, soon enough.

Now, he had no time to rest. He could take elixirs; they would give him the strength for the hurried return to his king. He rose and cracked the door.

Good. His faithful dog Sojel still stood guard.

"Sergeant." The stolid soldier turned attentively to his master. "We leave as soon as possible. Make things ready."

"Yes, my lord."

"And send Nafal to me."

~ ~ ~

"The rebec is not a difficult instrument."

"Easier than the harp?" asked Donzalo. He had been listening to his guest's idle strumming.

"Oh, aye, much easier. At least," continued the minstrel, "for the sort of thing I do. I should use a bow, of course, but I keep losing them. Now my friend, Oder – " He stopped, as if suddenly aware of what he had said.

"Oder. An Anian name."

"Yes. I shouldn't admit to having such friends in the heart of Lama."

The boy shrugged. "It is no concern of mine. But I would be cautious of announcing it outside these walls."

He has prejudices but tries to overcome them, thought Guesare. His casual reference to the hated Easterners had been dropped into their conversation to learn just this. He had suspected the boy to be open but it was good to be certain he would not reject the Ani unthinkingly.

"I shall be careful," he announced. "Oder, as I was saying, is a true master of the instrument. He can – what is it?"

Donzalo was staring into the corner. There, a circle of cold light was floating, growing, a ghastly, green halo.

At its center lay a hole into the darkest of hells.

13

"Quickly, lad, span and prime my pistols. They're already loaded." Guesare slid his heavy saber from its scabbard. "Hurry now!"

Donzalo drew forth the matched pair of wheel-locks, holstered on the minstrel's worn saddle. He had handled the handsome weapons admiringly earlier in the evening. The young Laman might be no fighter but fine craftsmanship and all things mechanical fascinated him. He measured out gunpowder for each and wound their springs.

"What is that?" he asked his companion. The circle continued to expand.

"A gateway. I doubt not that evil lies on its far side."

"Here are your pistols. Can't we get away?" Donzalo eyed the heavy door.

"It will be targeted to one of us. Most likely, you." The minstrel shook his head. "And will follow where'er you run."

"Best then I arm myself." The younger man stepped into his bedchamber, returning with a heavy spiked mace. "This needs little skill." He laughed nervously, then looked again to the door. "Even if this thing will indeed pursue me, might we not better face it in the open? With perhaps some help?"

He stepped forward and attempted to lift the bar. "It – it will not move." He struggled with the wooden beam. Donzalo believed in logic. His belief had let him down.

"You knew it would not," he accused.

"I suspected it would not. Radal is thorough. Stand ready!"

Something was stirring within the portal, now nearly a yard wide.

~ ~ ~

"My lord?"

"Come in, Nafal. We leave at once. Is all prepared?"

"Yes, my lord. Are you well, sir?" Jobareth was shocked by the man's appearance. "I mean, can you travel?"

"I must, so I can. Have you heard of anything unusual happening this night?"

"Here, sir? No, it has been as quiet as ever."

"Dead quiet, I hope." Radal smiled a brief, mirthless smile at his private joke. "Let's go. Bring the diplomatic bag."

The way was thankfully short. In the courtyard awaited Sergeant Sojel and his troop, horses and baggage ready. Sir Paren also stood there to give them an official goodbye, as well as to keep an official eye on them.

Although he wondered at the Sharshites' midnight departure, the knight was more than happy to see them go.

Slowly, stiffly, but by his own power, the envoy mounted. His young aide once started forward to help but a look from Sojel quickly warned him away. Radal would not allow himself to show weakness. The sergeant knew this, admired this: a godless man, he worshiped only his master.

Then they rode forth, silently, through the gates of Castle Rosam. Taking one last look back, Jobareth Nafal was certain that he glimpsed the Lady Lomela, watching from her balcony.

~ ~ ~

An eye. A pointed snout. The gleam of sharp teeth. Animals, several of them, but none that Donzalo had seen outside of nightmares.

"'Tis Jov's own fortune that you spied the light when you did," whispered his companion. "Had we been sleeping there would have been no chance."

"Do you know what they are?"

"Wart dogs."

The name brought forth a vague memory in the Laman's mind; he had read something, sometime. Of course, the hounds of Asak, God of Death. Bred in the mountains of Asa-Zad by that deity's priests.

"Weren't they exterminated when Asa-Zad fell?"

"I doubt these beasts were raised in this world at all. They may well come straight from Asak's realm." Guesare lifted a pistol. "I'll try to kill two before they come through. If there be time, reload for me."

There was no time; the beasts rushed forward at the first shot.

One never made it through the gateway. Another fell dead just inside the room.

They *are* dogs, thought Donzalo with brief surprise. Then he was swinging a mace with all the power inherent in his over-sized frame. Fortunately, his chambers had high ceilings, allowing a full motion; he had chosen them for their headroom.

He brought the weapon down on the powerful gibbous shoulders of the first misshapen beast to reach him, barely avoiding the curving tusks. Donzalo did not fail to note, despite his immediate concern with survival, that the entire pack had come toward him, not the minstrel.

He also did not fail to note that a blow to the shoulders was not overly effective – too much muscle there. The head made a better target.

Guesare fell upon the creatures with saber and abandonment, wisely cutting at their legs. A hamstrung wart dog posed little danger. One by one, in silence, the death god's pack bounded into the room. They began to form a ring around their intended victim, keeping just beyond reach of his deadly mace.

Fortunate it had been that Donzalo had picked up the unused weapon, when sorting through the armory with Copago one day. He had never thought to use it as more than a wall hanging.

"Back to back!" called Guesare.

Donzalo complied. "How many?" he gasped over his shoulder.

"Thirteen, of course," laughed the bard. "Four of them down."

The room was small and cramped; that was to the advantage of the men. They could not be effectively rushed by the entire pack. Indeed, the hounds barely had room to maneuver.

Donzalo saw his chance, lunged forward, and shattered the jaws of one.

"So you're a fighting man after all!" exclaimed Guesare.

"Not if I can help it," he grunted in reply. "Aah!"

A hound had slashed his leg with its tusks. Not without taking a saber in its side for its effort.

"My bedchamber! We can defend the doorway."

"Yes," the Cuddonian agreed. "Let's – "

"Go!" shouted Donzalo.

Swinging his weapon wildly, he cleared the way.

~ ~ ~

"No one seems to know how badly this minstrel is hurt."

"The Sharshite seemed to think he might not show at all," Perdos told his brother. "I got the impression he had his own plans for the fellow."

"I hope not. I want to kill him myself."

"I care not who kills him." He took another gulp from his tankard. "As long as he is dead."

Percos nodded. His brother might never again use his shattered arm, now in a sling. "Wouldn't it be better to lie down or something?"

"This damned arm hurts too much unless I sit. Pour me another, will you?"

"Sure. No more for me – want to be sharp in the morning."

"Good thinking, kid, you'd best get some sleep. But I intend to get as drunk as possible."

"Not too drunk, Dos," grinned the younger brother as he rose, "or you'll miss my skewering of the dog."

~ ~ ~

Donzalo bled; it made his boot soggy and most uncomfortable. The throbbing torture of the wound itself he attempted to ignore. He could not ignore the stiffening of his leg.

He stood ready now behind the minstrel, who defended the narrow doorway. Massive mace firmly in a two-handed grip, Donzalo was prepared to brain any beast that got past Guesare's sword.

It seemed an impasse. The wart dogs would lunge and snarl, but kept themselves away from that deadly blade. The Cuddonian knew he would tire soon. He knew also that Radal's spells would expire before long. Would he be able to last? Would he be able to withstand the inevitable charge?

For they would charge; their mission in this world meant more than their lives. They hungered for the blood and flesh and soul of Donzalo Rosam.

There was no door to shut against them – only a curtain had separated the rooms. Nor was there any furniture of convenient size to block the way. Their strength and their weapons would have to serve.

Then, suddenly, the pack stopped and withdrew, gathering themselves in silent menace. Seven remained standing; an eighth, entrails spilling on the floor, attempted to crawl forward to join its comrades.

"The rush is about to come," warned Guesare.

"Let it!"

14

"Radal and his entourage are gone," reported Paren. "Good riddance."

"You must be more practical, brother. Sharsh is our ally now."

"An ally I would never trust."

Borrago chuckled. "That is true of all allies. Lareth will certainly stand watching. Still," he continued, "our courses run together for the time."

He looked toward the door. There stood the master of arms, concern evident on his hawk-like visage.

"What is it, Copago?"

"Sir, there may be a problem with your son – Donzalo, that is." The soldier strode into the room to give his account. "A servant reported odd sounds coming from his chambers. When we investigated, it sounded like a struggle was taking place."

"Did you enter?" Borrago rose to his feet immediately, heading for the door.

"We could get no answer from within." He seemed perplexed. "The way was barred and our attempt to force it was without success."

"Wasn't Guesare with him, Paren?"

"Yes," replied the tall knight, hurrying down the hall on the heels of his brother. "I would expect no foul play from him."

"He might well be the target of such," interjected Copago.

"By Kamat, why couldn't that minstrel leave my boy alone?"

~ ~ ~

The silence of his adversaries disconcerted Guesare. A single snarl might make them seem more real, more capable of being vanquished.

Behind him, Donzalo assessed their foes. The bard would kill one, perhaps two, before he went down beneath their weight. Then the remainder into the small bedchamber; that would not do. He bent to speak into his companion's ear.

Guesare nodded agreement. As the first of the pack charged forward, he ducked beneath its leap. The younger man's club took it full aside the head, which nearly parted company with the hairless, nodose body. As quickly, the Cuddonian rose and ran this saber through the second in line.

Alas, he could not withdraw it from the beast's body. Seeing his predicament, Donzalo passed him the long recurved knife he normally bore on his belt; he was a nobleman and expected to carry a blade of some sort. For Guesare it was practically a short sword, with a full foot of edge.

At any rate, it was a far more effective armament than the dainty poniard at his own waist.

For a moment, only, the pack had been tangled in, and delayed by, its own dead. Now the remaining five came on. The first fell upon the minstrel, bearing both to the floor. Massive slobbering jaws snapped in the man's face as he disemboweled it.

Holding the mace like a battering ram, Donzalo charged the remaining dogs, crashing through them and into the other room. Though none were seriously harmed, their attack had been broken, scattered, and a young giant now stood among them, swinging his deadly spiked weapon.

One fell, its forelegs shattered; another took a blow that cost it an eye and made it wobble briefly. Yet it came on, its one instinct to taste the blood of the Laman. A blood-soaked Guesare struggled from beneath the mass of his dying attacker to behold the boy become of a sudden the man.

And he knew now with certainty what he had suspected: Donzalo would be not an ordinary man but a man of destiny.

~ ~ ~

"This way, sir."

"What? Donni changed his quarters?"

"He moved last year," answered Copago. "He's above the barracks now."

"My old rooms," added Paren.

"Oh, the high ceilings. Of course." Borrago again took the lead, with quick, purposeful strides.

A knot of soldiers waited at the barred door. "What report?" barked the master of arms.

"There is still commotion inside," answered their sergeant. "We heard no speech," he continued, laying his hand on the heavy oak door, "and we can not force this with the strength of our shoulders. I sent for a ram."

"Not much room to use one," Paren pointed out.

"Axes!" commanded Borrago. "Chop that door to splinters."

Copago nodded. "Go." The sergeant motioned for two of his men to follow and hurried off.

"I do not like this, my lord." The master of arms gestured toward the entrance. "Not at all. This door should not be so difficult to break down. I know the lad has only a light bar on it."

"You and I," Paren said to him, nodding in its direction. "Maybe with my weight we can budge it."

"Very well, sir. On three!"

At the count, the two men slammed their shoulders into the door, which literally flew from its hinges. Copago and Paren sprawled atop the fallen panel.

"Hello, Uncle," came the cheerful greeting of Donzalo. He was seated in a battered chair, foot propped upon the most hideous creature the knight had ever beheld. "Hello, Master Copago."

Borrago stepped around his brother's prone form. "Are you all right, boy? And what, by all the ice in hell, is that – are these?" he asked, surveying the bodies that littered the room.

"These were a parting gift from Sharsh," spoke a weary and blood-stained Guesare, rising from a corner, "which we must discuss. But first, Cousin, this brave lad needs a physician."

~ ~ ~

"The wound is not bad, sire," reported Doctor Heragos. He pulled at the thin tuft of beard adorning his chin. "But I know not what poisons might lie in yon jaws." The young man, recently come from a Siphic school, shook his head at the sight of the gruesome corpses, now piled to one side of the chamber.

"All I can do is wash it thoroughly with brandywine and stitch it up."

"There is a healing virtue to brandywine?" queried Guesare, always a man of curiosities and interests.

"Not truly, sir, any strong liquor seems to prevent the growth of poisons. The potent drink the peasants here make from corn should work quite as well."

"Ah," Paren observed, "just as it will preserve fruit and such."

"Then Bolos need never fear poisoning," laughed Donzalo. "Ow!" The doctor was vigorously cleansing his hurt.

"My lord, we'd best dispose of these carcasses," Copago pointed out.

"Far from the keep," suggested the minstrel, "and buried deep. Hmm, I must remember that rhyme." He looked to his erstwhile comrade in arms. "I intend to immortalize our battle, my friend.

"Kinsman Borrago, your younger son is a warrior true."

"So I see," answered the count, "so I see. You have done well yourself – Cousin."

Donzalo was gritting his teeth and ignoring Heragos, now busy with needle and thread. "Guesare must fight again in a few hours," he reminded the group.

"Yes," exclaimed Borrago, "I'd forgotten! Physician, see to this man when you finish there." His voice became stern, his eyes narrowed in reproof. "I expect an explanation of all this when you finish your duel, young fellow," he told the bard. Then he chuckled. "So be sure you win!"

~ ~ ~

"Wake up, Brother."

"What? Damn, my arm! Don't shake me like that!"

"It's dawn. Time to go."

"Is Jak here?"

"Right here," announced the man in question, a burly, balding soldier. "Ready to be his second."

"Good, let's go. Any word on the Cuddonian?"

"There was some sort of commotion," Jak reported, "but I saw the dog a short time ago. Looked tired."

"Did he seem hurt?" asked Percos.

The soldier shook his head.

Grumbled Perdos, "Too bad."

"It's okay, Dos, I'll hurt him good," his brother promised. The trio headed for the castle gate; all duels must be held outside the triple ring of walls.

"Anyone know if the boss is coming?" asked Jak.

"Bolos? I doubt it." Percos spat. "He doesn't give the shit in his bowels about any of us."

"No lord does, Cos. We just take their money and do our job."

The younger brother nodded. "As long as it suits us."

"Aye."

Jak looked from the one to the other as they strolled through the second gateway. "You two are a hard lot, aren't you? I like the young lord."

Perdos snickered. "Like him all you like, but don't trust him."

"Third gate is still closed," said Percos. "We'll have to wait."

"Ho, sluggards," called his brother to the soldiers manning the wall, "why didn't you open at dawn?"

"Count's orders," their leader announced. "Something's going on up at the keep."

15

"I could order this duel be canceled," the count told Guesare, "or postponed."

"It must be now, if ever. I should be away and so should your son. He is not safe remaining here. And," continued the minstrel, "I do not wish to leave a dangerous and vengeful enemy behind."

"You do not think that these Northerners were involved in last night's doings? If they had aught to do with it, I'll hang them from the walls."

"No, Cousin, though I've no doubt they are in the pay of Sharsh. 'Twould raise awkward questions if you acted against them directly. Best I slay one; that sends a more subtle message."

Borrago smoothed his mustache, a habit when he became thoughtful. "Yes, it is best that I not acknowledge the attack openly. But, damn it, Guesare, they almost killed my boy! And you too." He looked at his kinsman questioningly as they rode down toward the outer wall. "Which of you was the intended target, I know not."

"I will tell all after this business, if I can. But should I fail today, get the lad to some safe place. 'Twas he Lareth wants gone." He glanced ahead, spying the trio standing at the gate. "My opponent awaits us."

"Copago!" called the count over his shoulder. "Go tell Sergeant Ubos to open up." The master of arms galloped ahead, leaving a pair of his most trusted men to guard their master. Paren had remained at the keep, left the task of quietly disposing of twelve deceased wart dogs.

Donzalo, despite his objections, had also stayed behind, resting in well-guarded safety.

Out they rode, now, through the open gateway and into the green countryside, into a fresh spring morning. Borrago ignored the three men on foot as he passed.

~~~

"What's up here, lads?" rasped Jak. "Why is the count with yon minstrel?"
~~~

"They're kinsmen," came Perdos's nonchalant answer.

"Everyone knows that," added Percos.

But the look the two brothers exchanged betrayed their nervousness. "We've been found out," the younger man whispered.

"Maybe so. Play it cool."

They followed the mounted contingent to a field not far from the gates, a bit of pasture that had long served as dueling ground. The two groups stopped a short distance apart.

Jak stepped forward to fulfill his duties as second. Copago did the same. The two men spoke briefly but Percos could not make out the words. Instead, he found himself listening to a mocking bird on the far side of the meadow.

For a moment, he thought he heard his name in its song.

"Wake up, fool," hissed his brother. "Here comes the count's bastard."

Solemnly, Copago announced, "Guesare sends his greetings and his defiance. Draw your sword and may Kamat be with you."

~ ~ ~

Borrago loved his natural son, an indiscretion of his youth, every bit as much as his legitimate children, yet he always had difficulty showing the affection he felt for Copago. His pride, however, was obvious.

The two stood now, side by side, the younger man a mirror of the older.

"I pray Guesare's injuries do not prove his undoing here."

"He received none yesterday, sir."

The count raised an eyebrow. "Indeed?"

"The minstrel faked his hurts. He could have faced me for another tilt."

"Not the action of a gentleman, eh?"

"I would have done the same, my lord."

"As would I, Copago, as would I. He did not seem to take any harm during last night's adventure."

The master of arms shook his head. "No, sir, but he is bound to be sore and tired from both that affair and the jousting. Percos seems fresh."

The combatants approached each other, swords at the ready. Guesare held his saber. A longer straight sword was in the hands of his opponent.

"So," mused Borrago, "Guesare's speed will suffer. One of his main assets."

"And his stamina, sir. He might normally have hoped to wear his man down."

"Yes. He will need to be bold."

The duelists circled cautiously, neither risking an attack. Guesare seemed to move slowly, painfully.

"The sly trickster! He's still acting the wounded man."

"Yes," agreed Copago, "but it will give him only one chance to surprise his foe."

"The longer he can wait, the better it will work," observed the count. "Who is this?" A horseman approached.

"It is your son, my lord."

A bleary-eyed Bolos cantered up. He remained astride his mount, watching the fight.

Encouraged by his opponent's apparent condition, Percos took the initiative. The bard backed slowly away from his onslaught.

"Guesare can not do that for long," Borrago stated.

Guesare did not need to. The larger man, veteran and victor of many such combats, allowed his confidence to become over-confidence. He aimed a sweeping two-handed blow, knowing his strength should overwhelm an injured opponent. And in doing so, Percos left an opening, so brief an opening, yet all the Cuddonian required. Then, as in the case of most duels, it was quickly over.

The body of Percos slid from the saber that had pierced his chest. As he died, on that fine spring morn, he again heard the mocking bird sing his name.

~ ~ ~

With an oath, Perdos slipped his dagger from its sheath.

"Hold there," growled Jak, grasping his arm. "Do not be a fool."

Bolos alit beside them and gave Jak an approving nod. "We'd best gather up yon unfortunate. Use my horse."

As a brooding Perdos watched, he and the stolid soldier loaded the corpse onto his steed, covering it over with the tattered and stained cloak Percos had shrugged off a few minutes earlier. Jak led it off toward the castle. "Come along, man," said Bolos, putting a hand on the bereaved brother's shoulder. "There is no more to be done."

"Not now," spat Perdos, giving Guesare a look of hatred. "Not now," he repeated, the words almost a whisper, and followed his brother home.

The bard was calmly cleaning his blade. Guesare was a man of moods. The earlier elation had given way a great weariness, a let-down now that this affair had reached its anticlimactic end. He mumbled a short prayer for the soul of Percos and meant it.

Slowly, the minstrel returned to the others. "My Lord Cousin," said he, addressing Borrago, "I ask for your patience. I will tell you all I know, but now I fear I need sleep."

16

"It is decided, then," declared the count. "Donzalo will go to live with his uncle for now." Paren nodded his agreement.

"And Guesare will accompany him. I do not understand your involvement in this, Cousin, nor fully the reasons Lareth wishes my boy dead. But I thank you for your aid."

"I think, my lord, that I am attaching myself to a rising star." Borrago seemed amused by the minstrel's new-found respectfulness to him – and to his son. "The young man needs learn much. Between us, your brother and I can teach him well."

For the first time in this council, Bolos spoke. "It amazes me that this whole affair was going on under my unsuspecting nose." He gave a rueful laugh. "I was in my cups far too much of the time.

"It also seems I have greatly underestimated you, Brother," the nobleman told Donzalo, "as well as my wife. Are you sure she is to be trusted?"

"As much as anyone in this room," the younger man averred. He sat to one side, his wounded leg propped on a stool. "And her friend, Nafal, too – I believe."

"Very well. Perdos has already told me he is leaving my service. I will need not dismiss him.

"He will neither forget nor forgive you, minstrel." From his manner of address, it seemed that Bolos still felt a certain distaste for the Cuddonian.

Guesare shrugged. "So be it. I will deal with that scum when the time comes.

"And when, sir," he asked Borrago," will the time come for us to depart?"

"Give the boy some time to heal and prepare himself. A week."

~ ~ ~

"Guesare says he will give me the full explanation once we are on the road. I think – " Donzalo hesitated. "I think it is something he does not wish you to know."

"There are those things we do not wish him to know," replied a smiling Lomela. They looked out over the courtyard, as the evening breeze toyed with the lady's auburn hair.

The young man returned the smile. "We all have our secrets."

"I will miss you, Donni. Is the leg truly healed?"

"Yes, Lomela, and we must go on the morrow. I will miss you as well, my princess."

"I have dismissed Traspa for the night. Stay with me."

~ ~ ~

By mid-morn, they were leagues from the keep. Donzalo rode silently by Guesare's side, a short distance behind his aunt and uncle. His thoughts were many but foremost was the knightly bard's promised explanation. He could contain himself no longer.

"Sir?"

Guesare gave a small smile. "You await my story."

Not certain whether this was a question, Donzalo nodded.

"You have heard of the oracle at Cars." He paused briefly; again his companion nodded.

"In Lorj," he said.

"Yes. The oracle is never wrong – ambiguous at times, as oracles are wont to be, but never wrong. Before the birth of your nephew, King Lareth sent a secret envoy to Cars, to pay the price and ask his question."

"Uh, Guesare, how do you know of this? I mean, if it was secret?"

"I have friends who are well rewarded to learn such things. Nations other than Sharsh employ agents.

"Anyway, the question was this: 'What future awaits the first born of Lomela?' 'Twas worded thus because Bolos already had several bastards. One must be careful of such things when questioning an oracle.

"The reply Lareth received may not have directly answered his query, yet it was straightforward enough. Cars prophesied that the son of Donzalo would rule in Lama."

Guesare rode on in silence, allowing the boy to think about this a while. Then he spoke.

"Now such a statement could be interpreted many ways. Your son, perhaps, could be a vassal of young Ros, holding lands in feality, or you might win yourself new holdings in the East, or even marry into some other landed family. But, taking the worst view, he saw you as a threat to his grandson's future. After all, the question had been about the babe.

"The fool! He went seeking the future, only to reject what he found. He must need make the attempt, even knowing that it would fail, and try to remove you."

Unexpectedly, Donzalo smiled, then suppressed a giggle.

"That is not the response I expected from you," said the minstrel, puzzled.

"It is only that I understand the oracle."

Guesare waited for him to explain.

"You see, Lomela and Bolos didn't really like each other very much. My brother is somewhat older than his wife and, I think, prefers women of a coarser sort. And then, he was often gone from Castle Rosam, and Lomela and I found ourselves together a great deal and became close and so – "

"So? Ah!" he exclaimed, in sudden enlightenment. "So Ros is your son and will someday rule as the oracle predicts." The Easterner broke into laughter, but sobered suddenly.

"Does Bolos know this?"

"I am sure he has no suspicions. My brother has trouble keeping track of whom he bedded when, especially if he has been drinking."

"This does not change the danger to you, boy. Old King Lareth still wants your blood." Guesare reflected a moment. "It does change your situation with regards to me and my friends. Yet I think you will be useful, even so, perhaps even more than before. Be that as it may, I am not the sort to abandon one I have promised aid."

"Then you intend to remain?"

"Indeed, I shall. I've not only duty but friendship to hold me. Let's ride, Donni; it is a long road ahead."

OF ROADS: THE SECOND TALE

1

Morparas stank; it reeked of refuse and tide flats, of fish and of fires burning on ten thousand hearths. The stench did not trouble Sojel. He liked this town with its fleshpots and taverns, as much as he liked any place in his world.

The man across the table from him he despised as a fool.

"You're from Mura, aren't you?" asked his companion. He only nodded. He had no intention of telling this fellow why he had left his home.

Perdos shrugged his broad shoulders, one rising higher than the other. It wasn't hard for him to guess that Sojel had worn out his welcome in most of the places he had been. Let the saturnine sergeant keep his silence. He did not care for this knife-blade of a man anyway.

"Any new orders from your master?" he asked.

"None. He sought only a report."

"Humph. I do wish he'd let me act. I would dearly love to skewer that minstrel."

Sojel's sneer told of his contempt for the Laman's abilities. "You did poorly enough the last time you tried. Wait for orders."

"I'm sick of waiting!" Perdos was as quick to anger as ever. "I care naught for the boy nor for your wizard. If he does not say to act soon I'll do it myself."

"The chance will come. Bide your time, man, and keep up the watch." The sergeant drained his tankard. "I need a woman. What say we find a couple?"

"The best idea I've heard this evening. Don't mistreat yours," he warned the soldier. "I don't need any trouble here."

~ ~ ~

"Finesse! Finesse!" scolded Guesare. "Do not depend so much on your strength."

Paren chuckled. "The lad is already a far better swordsman than I."

"Perhaps you should have some lessons as well, Uncle."

"One over-sized pupil is quite enough! What news, Sir Paren?" The knight had watched their practice patiently but his desire to interrupt had been obvious.

"You are to be an uncle again, Donni. The Lady Lomela is with child."

The bard and his protege exchanged a meaningful look. "Um, good news, Uncle Paren. Any word on my brother?" asked Donazalo.

"Your father seems very pleased with Bolos these days. He drinks far less and apparently takes his husbandly duties seriously."

"That is well," commented Guesare, absently stroking his golden beard. "'Twill soon be winter; we'd best be making plans."

Donzalo shrugged off his jack-coat. "I want to see my home," he declared. "Harvest Feast comes soon."

"Celebrate with your aunt and me, boy. I don't like the idea of you being on the road, even with Sir Guesare's skills to protect you." Paren's concern, and his love for his nephew, was plain. "There have been too many reports of strangers skulking about lately."

"I have seen them, myself," said the minstrel, "and have little doubt that they are here to spy on Donzalo, perhaps to do him mischief. He well might be safer wintering at Castle Rosam. Or," he added, "in the Cuddon."

"Your home?" The young man was surprised.

"Aye. We celebrate the Yule properly in the hills!"

"Well," spoke Paren, "I'll have to give this some thought. Tonight we will speak further on it." He turned abruptly and strode away, leaving the two in their sheep pen turned fencing ground.

"Your uncle does not wish to see you go." Guesare turned to his young friend and spoke in a low and serious voice. "I thought the princess wrote to you."

"Yes, frequently. She never mentioned this."

"The child is your brother's?"

"I do not know."

~ ~ ~

"Hello, Jobo."

"My Lady Fachalana." Jobareth turned toward a shadowed bench.

"My lady?" asked the young woman, rising to her full and considerable height. "Why so formal?"

"In the home of your father, it seems wise."

Fachalana was of an age with Nafal and, by any standards, striking. "You were never so in the past. I thought you liked me," she teased, her expression thoroughly theatrical.

"Certainly, my lady," he replied, but sounded quite uncertain.

"Ah, but you've always had the hots for Lomela." His blush brought a gentle and only slightly mocking, laugh. "Don't deny it, Jobo."

"Yes," he admitted, "but she has married, as princesses must. She knew her duty. And," the young diplomat added, "I knew mine."

Fachalana laughed again and tossed back the black hair she allowed to fall free upon her shoulders. "And I don't? I'll marry if and when I please, and not to suit my father's ambitions." A sly and somewhat wicked smile found its way to her face. "I wonder what he would think of you as a choice."

"I think, my lady," said he, falling into a pattern of easy banter, "that the Lord Radal would applaud any choice now."

"Nicely parried! Did you know," she asked, changing the direction of their conversation, "that I have been studying the sword?"

"No more acting?"

"Oh, yes. I wanted to use a blade convincingly on stage. However, I must admit that I enjoy fencing." The young noblewoman continued with genuine pride. "I can best most of the other students. I have educated more than one well-bred boy!"

"I do not doubt it, Lana. You always threw yourself into whatever you chose to do."

"Are you on your way to Father?"

"Yes. He called for my presence. I know not why."

"He plans to travel to the East," she confided.

"To Lama?"

"Only to the mountains." A dramatic pause was necessary; they often were in Fachalana's speech. "But you will go further."

"Then an embassy is being sent at last," mused Jobareth. "You seem to know a great deal."

"I pay attention." The serious and the jesting mingled themselves in her voice. "You would do well to cultivate me, Jobo."

"Indeed. Yet it seems, alas, that I shall soon be far away." It was his turn to tease.

"Behave yourself or I won't tell you who the ambassador is to be."

Nafal gave a nonchalant shrug. "I'm sure your father will let me know, soon enough."

"Well then, I shall beat the great Lord Radal!" the impatient Fachalana declared. Then she leaned close and whispered, "Lord Doufan."

A picture of an affable, middle-aged courtier came to his mind. "Very much the nonentity he promised. I'd best go, Lana. It is not good to keep your father waiting." He kissed her hand. "Thank you, my lady."

"You're very welcome, Jobareth. I do like you, you know, and wish you weren't going off to live with those barbarians." Her tone changed from the wistful to the impish. "Use the time to write a play for me – if Lomela doesn't keep you too busy."

~ ~ ~

"I will miss Donni," admitted Thara, "but six months is a long stay. He should at least visit his home."

Paren nodded his agreement. "I fear for his safety on the road. There is too much that needs my attention here or I would accompany them."

"You know fully well, husband mine, that I can run this manor without you."

These were the words he had hoped to hear. The knight valued his wife's approval. "I suppose I could make it there and back in a week."

"Take a fortnight – and do not include your time on the road in that! If you stay long enough he may decide to return with you."

He absently toyed with his cup. "I'll ask Borri to mention that idea to him. Still, once the boy is home, it may be the safest place for him to winter. I can't see him going off to the Cuddon!"

"It might not hurt Donni to travel some come the spring. Guesare seems an able protector."

"Aye. I'll miss him as well. Never thought to be saying that!" He chuckled. "I think a certain stable boy will miss him too."

"Perhaps we should be grateful he has such tastes. The last minstrel to stay here left half the serving maids with child." The Lady Thara had no problem being blunt. "Donzalo hasn't shown interest in any of the women here, has he?"

"Not that I've noticed. I think, my dear," he told her with a wink, "he takes after his old uncle and is waiting for the right one to come along."

2

"Ah, Blen. Enter!"

"Sire." The knight, who had hesitated at the doorway, stepped forward and bowed to his king.

Lareth regarded the man a moment. Sir Blen seemed a person of little significance, quiet and unassuming, yet he had served well as a courier some three years now, often in dangerous circumstances. The king motioned him to a seat and noted his awkwardness in accepting it.

"You are not comfortable around your king." He smiled thinly and added, "Nor around people in general, are you?" Lareth did not wait on an answer. "But on your own, you are a quite capable fellow. I have seen the reports."

"Um – thank you, Sire." Blen most certainly was uncomfortable.

"And most have, therefore, underestimated you. Even my Lord Radal." He was briefly amused by the man's reaction to that name. "You should, on the merits of your deeds, have seen advancement long before."

"I have no complaints, Highness," the knight blurted. "I like my position. I like being on the road."

"I'm sure you do, but you can hide there no longer. I have plans for you, Sir Blen. Plans, indeed! Come, walk with me."

The King of Sharsh stepped out through a stone archway, onto the eastward-facing battlements, the very spot where this man had brought him news some six months earlier. "Can you be loyal to me, Blen? To me and to none other?"

"Yes, Sire. To – to whom else could I be loyal?"

"You might be surprised at how divided ones loyalties can be."

"Not mine, my king. I am yours entirely." Blen certainly meant it, at least at that moment of enthusiasm.

"Then I call on you to take on a new post in my service. You will accompany my delegation to County Rosam, not as courier but as master of arms." Lareth gazed in the direction of that Laman court. "You know the area and the people. You know how to take care of yourself. Now," he continued, "I ask you to care for my envoys as well."

"I am honored, your Highness. Am I then, um, under the orders of Lord Doufan?"

"In name, Doufan is in charge. In fact, his secretary Nafal will probably run things. This," stated the king, "is why I need a man such as you there, one who will answer directly to me rather than being a creature of Radal.

"I trust the loyalty and motives of Lord Radal, but not always his methods and secrecy. And I believe Jobareth Nafal to be a decent young fellow. My daughter certainly does." He smiled at the thought, remembering the happy days when Lomela was a girl, playing with Jobareth in his gardens. How courtly the boy had tried to be, and how he had tried so to please his princess! Then the king continued. "I must trust you to keep an eye on things, to report to me privately what you see and what you think. Everything. Do you understand?"

"Yes, Sire." He paused a moment. "I am to be your spy."

"Just be who you already are, Sir Blen – a man no one notices but who notices everything."

~ ~ ~

"Tell me, Guesare, do you think I should grow a mustache?"

"'Twould make that great nose of yours seem all the larger," opined the minstrel. "Go for the full beard, my boy."

"And look like Uncle Paren? I think not!"

"Well, you've a good start there. Will you shave it all off when we reach the keep?"

Donzalo rubbed at his bristling chin. "I suppose it would be best. It is not the style. Not," he continued, looking at his companion's curling whiskers, "among those in my circle back home, anyway."

"Merchants who ape the court fashions of Sharsh."

The younger man nodded. "It is important to them to appear sophisticated. They are new to their power and know not whether they are nobles or tradesmen."

"Hmmph. I'd set them straight." Guesare had both a nobleman's and an artist's disdain for merchants.

Donazalo was quiet for a few moments, looking about him as they rode on. There was a taste of autumn in the air and most of the trees had begun to turn. Here they were coming out of a patch of forest and into more open farmland. It would not be far now to home.

"Speaking of appearances," he said, "do you think our escort will show itself?"

"Oh, you noted them, did you? Three men, I think."

"So did I count them. The tallest one might be our old friend Perdos."

"Only spies, I assume." The minstrel showed no concern. "If they meant mischief it would have happened before now, when there was more cover. And we do outnumber them." He glanced back at their companions, Paren and a pair of men-at-arms. Donzalo's uncle had been unwilling to spare more men from his manor at harvest time.

"I suspect that Perdos would love to send an arrow your direction."

"And I suspect he has orders otherwise," replied Guesare. "We'll be at Castle Rosam by nightfall and it will no longer matter."

~ ~ ~

Jobareth shut the heavy iron-bound door behind him.

"We are ready, then?" asked Sir Blen, who had apparently been waiting for him in the hall.

"Yes, Blen." The young man had decided to regard and treat this knight as an equal, as they officially shared a second-in-command status, and Blen had chosen to respond in kind. It would make things easier for both. "We can ride in the morning."

His companion nodded as they started down the hallway. "Any last minute changes, Lector?"

"None. We but went over a few details." He gave his companion a sidelong glance. "You know, Sir Blen, my master does not know quite what to make of you. It is unusual enough for him to be taken by surprise, as he was by your appointment." He stopped and looked squarely at the man. "But he does not know who you are. I think he paid you no attention until the king named you.

"And that," he chuckled, "is a puzzle as well."

"Shh," warned Blen, placing his hand on the younger man's shoulder. Striding toward them was Lord Radal's man, Sojel. He passed them wordlessly, not deigning to glance in their direction.

"No puzzle about him," said the knight. "He's on his way to get his own orders from your master."

Jobareth nodded. "Let us be hope those orders take him the way opposite of ours."

"Agreed. Indeed, I would wish that they take him straight to hell."

3

The outer wall of Castle Rosam, that portion nearest the first gate, was an earthen berm, surmounted by low stone walls. In the days of Borrago's childhood, there had been a wooden palisade but the count had, stone by stone, strengthened his walls as he had increased his wealth and power. Further down the ramparts on each side, where the hill grew steeper, the walls became all stone, eventually merging with the natural rock cliffs.

"What a fine day it is, Uncle!" Donzalo urged his mount forward and galloped through the open timber gate.

"It is a fine day," said Guesare to Paren, as they followed more sedately. "A fine autumn day and a fine day to return home. I've been thinking of my own home, lately."

The older man only nodded. He was already starting to miss his wife and manor.

"Where is the boy headed?" wondered the minstrel. For better defensibility, the gates of the three walls did not line up. After passing through the outer entrance, one had to turn to his right and go some distance laterally before reaching the second.

And, having passed that gate, one need turn back to the left and follow the path to the main portal into the castle itself. Donzalo, however, was heading straight ahead to the wall.

"The boy's in a hurry," laughed Paren. "They will let him down a ladder and he'll be home before we pass the second gate."

Already, a wooden ladder was being lowered; it was always kept at that spot on the walls for those in a hurry.

"Someone will come down to get Donni's horse. Oh, no need. It has decided to come with us." The riderless steed cantered up to them, where one of Paren's men took hold of its halter.

The lawn between the two outer walls was fairly broad. Outsiders were allowed into this area – but no further – to sell to those within the keep and, too, tents would rise here when the keep overflowed with guests. Mostly, though, it was used for training and sport. As the party approached the second gate and its iron portcullis, set between two towers in the rough stone wall, a voice rang out.

"Hail, Sir Paren! The count awaits you. How went the journey?"

Paren looked up to where Copago leaned out over the wall. "Well enough, Sir Copago, and hail to you. Is there any news I should know?"

"Nay, sir, it has been a quiet season. We do expect a delegation from Sharsh soon."

The knight exchanged a telling look with Guesare and, with a wave, rode on through the gateway.

~ ~ ~

Sojel was not easy on horses. He pushed them as he pushed his underlings, as he pushed himself. He had ridden hard through the night, the cold mountain night, beneath a hunters' moon, while behind him, even as it was setting, the official delegation to the court of Count Ros had prepared to depart. Now, fresh horse after fresh horse, day and night, he had pulled far ahead of them, catching a snatch of sleep in the saddle, ever speeding eastward.

Ahead, lay the rendezvous to which his master had dispatched him.

Never a man given to deep thoughts, Sojel neither knew nor cared about the reasons for his orders. They were his orders; that was enough.

Still, his mind wandered into many strange places as he rode. Most were locales we would not wish to visit. He also thought upon the envoys he was leaving ever further behind. Who was this Blen, anyway? Sojel recognized that the man disliked him and fully returned the sentiment. He and young Nafal had best not get between him and his task.

As the horizon before him began to dimly foretell another dawn, he passed from the hill country and, soon, turned aside from the main road into a wood. The river, and Ros-town beyond it, were not far further down that road, but his destination lay near at hand.

"Who goes there?" a voice barked from the darkness.

"Your master, dog," he curtly replied.

"Ah, Sergeant. You made good time, sir."

Sojel only grunted in reply, swinging down from his steed and handing the reins to the man. “Are all within?”

“Aye, sir.”

“See that my horse is well rubbed down.” Sojel might use his tools hard but he also knew to take good care of them, after. He turned to a hut hidden away in this grove, a hint of light coming from around its door. More light than he would have permitted, had he been here earlier. Now it mattered little.

A rough-looking group awaited him inside, three men including the Laman, Perdos. All were awake and huddled about a small fire pit, the smoke of which passed out through a hole in the cobweb-shrouded ceiling.

Or mostly passed out – the hut itself reeked of it and the filth of the occupants. Sojel addressed them. “We have orders. Gather ’round.”

“Should we call in Van?” asked one, a moon-faced scoundrel. His moon-face included more than a few craters.

“Nay, he is tending my horse.” Vanob was the one man here in whom Sojel put any trust whatsoever, being one of his soldiers rather than a common ruffian like these three. He could fill him in later, if need be.

“The time is come,” said Sojel, “to remove the young lordling Donzalo, now he is returned to his father’s keep. You,” he nodded toward Perdos, “will have to sit it out. You are too well known around Borrago’s holdings.”

The Laman scowled but said nothing. After all, he thought, I care nothing about the boy. There will be a chance at that Cuddonian when this business is done.

“Asak made you two for this sort of thing anyway,” he told the others. “Now here’s the plan.”

~ ~ ~

Donzalo bounded up the stairs, his long legs taking two or three risers at a time. He would see his father later; time enough for that!

Right now, he had other affairs to attend. Yet, as he reached the door to Lady Vibola's room, he paused, suddenly uncertain.

A waylaid page had assured him the Lady Lomela was with his grandmother. But would she want to see him? Perhaps he should have waited, cleaned off the dust of the road, seen his father. Oh, well. He shrugged and knocked at the panel.

He did not know the serving girl who answered and she, apparently, did not know who he was. Fresh from the farm, Donzalo thought to himself, and getting a quick education from Grandmother.

"You may tell the Lady Vibola that her grandson is calling."

"Oh, is that Donni? Let him in, silly girl!"

He smiled at her as she opened wide the door and took his travel-soiled cloak. Life is probably hard enough for her as it is, the young man thought, and it never hurts one to be pleasant. He couldn't help note that she was rather pretty, too, being, as we just mentioned, a young man.

"Welcome home," spoke Lomela, who sat beside the old woman. "We have both missed you."

Donzalo now noted the changes in both these women. Lomela was only obviously pregnant to one who already knew. Five months, perhaps, he thought. Not mine.

It was the Lady Vibola whose appearance jarred him. She looked far older, far less the vibrant matriarch he had left two seasons ago. "Grandmother." He knelt down to embrace and kiss her. "I have very much missed you." He looked up and gave the younger woman a smile. "You too, of course, my Lady Lomela."

And suddenly found tears in his eyes.

4

The troop was small that rode from Mountain Keep that early morning. Along with its two leaders came a pair of attendants and four soldiers, all former comrades of Blen in the eastern command. Their mission was only to pave the way for the ambassador, Lord Doufan, who would follow in the spring.

Unlike the man who had, unknown to them, preceded their group down this road, Sir Blen and Lector Jobareth Nafal were in no hurry. There was no urgency to their work and it was fine autumn weather, dry and cool. Blen looked back at the castle.

"You are a scholar," he said to his companion, "where I know only the tales told in barracks and bars."

Jobareth nodded, though he suspected that the knight was more knowledgeable than he was admitting.

"This castle back here, it belonged to the Rosam at one time, didn't it?"

"Hmm, well, they weren't called the Rosam then, in that Count Ros was son to the man who ruled there. But yes, it was that family."

Blen looked at him expectantly and Nafal, who had no objections to lecturing, took his cue. "Back in the days of the short-lived Anian occupation of Sharsh, an adventurer, or freedom fighter, some might say," both men smiled at that, knowing what they did of politics, "set himself up as an independent power in the mountains. That was Paren, who styled himself a duke."

"The father of Ros."

"Right. He had three other sons, all of whom died in battle, but Ros had been sent eastward to Lama to seek out allies. Instead, he married into them. Actually," continued the lector, "there were daughters as well, who married into the Sharshite nobility. Their descendants are now a part of the court."

"Despite the fact that Lareth's father murdered most of the family," mused the knight.

"King Greneth had only succeeded in driving the Ani out and could not permit this independent power to sit on his border. Moreover, Paren had taken a wife from the old royalty and could well have challenged him for the throne.

"It was treachery that undid Duke Paren, a traitor who opened a gate for the king's men. They slew the three sons but the old man himself escaped into the east. And since," he concluded, "the keep has been a bulwark of Sharsh, defending the main mountain pass in this region and the eastern border."

"That means," said Blen, with a sudden insight, "that Count Borrago and his clan have not only a claim on the Mountain Keep and its surrounds, but also on the throne itself." He whistled softly. "This, I did not know."

"I'm sure King Lareth knows it very well," replied Jobareth Nafal.

~ ~ ~

"It looks like storm weather moving in," observed Sir Paren.

Borrago only nodded absently but Guesare looked to the grey northern horizon. "It's already to the upper Cuddon, I'd say. There might even be snow."

"Far too early for that here." Paren, none the less, looked a bit worried. His manor was on his mind, as often before and, no doubt, many times to come.

They were gathered atop the tower that stood at the center of Castle Rosam. Borrago liked to sit up here, the highest point in the keep, and think on things. Now, it seemed as good a place as any to hold a council, as long as the threatening weather held off.

His sons were here – the two legitimate ones – and Paren and Guesare. He had considered including his other son. He had even considered the Lady Lomela, yet still had reservations as to her loyalties. Best to keep it to these five, felt Borrago. Let others in later, if need be.

"How do we greet the delegation from Sharsh," he asked the group, "considering what happened the last time one was here?" Borrago looked directly at Donzalo.

"I count Jobareth Nafal a friend," his son replied, "and would welcome him as such."

"And that is, of course, good diplomacy," added Guesare, with the slightest of shrugs.

"Have we any idea who is accompanying the young lector?" asked Paren, ever quick to get to practical questions.

"Yes, Brother. Do you recall the courier Blen?"

Paren nodded. "A decent fellow, seemingly," he allowed.

"He's to be their master of arms and would, I assume, have the running of the household. We could do far worse than having him and Nafal here. Naturally," Borrago continued, "we can assume a spy among their retinue."

"Only one?" quipped Guesare.

Bolos had been pacing the weathered plank floor. "How," he asked, speaking up at last, "can we act as if nothing occurred? We all know the Sharshites want my brother dead. I say turn them away!"

"What is that cliche, Guesare? Keep your friends close and your enemies closer?"

"That's it, Cousin Borrago. But not close enough to slip a knife into one, I would hope."

Bolos harrumphed. "The only harmless enemy is a dead one."

"We can't kill all of Sharsh, Bolos." Paren shook his head. "Best to pretend that what everyone knows happened, didn't. At least for now."

The other three murmured their agreement and Bolos shrugged in acquiescence.

"So," continued the count, "our other business: what do we do with Donzalo now?"

"Donzalo has his own ideas about that," stated the person in question.

"Why don't you come back to the manor with me?" asked Paren. "There's more to do and learn and you may well be reeve there when I am gone. Assuming, " he bowed toward Bolos, "the count at that time so wishes."

"Don't assume you'll outlive me, Parri," growled his older brother. "I'm not sure it's safer for him than right here."

"The walls of Castle Rosam were no defense last time," Guesare reminded them. "But then, neither would be Sir Paren's keep. By the way, my lord," he turned toward the knight and hesitated slightly before speaking, "I took the liberty of leaving a few charms of protection behind, just in case someone attempted magics while we were gone."

Paren looked askance at the minstrel, but only for a moment. "Perhaps that is well. I thank you for protecting the Lady Thara."

Guesare nodded. "They would be useless against the sort of attack Radal unleashed here but they might block smaller evils."

"Is it possible to ward this castle?" asked Bolos.

"Again, only against small magics. Yet, truly, it is unlikely that a powerful sorcerer would get close enough to do harm now that we are on the guard. Certainly, we wouldn't let Radal through the gates again!"

Donzalo laughed. "So all I have to do is lock myself in this tower for the rest of my life."

"That would work," came Guesare's dry reply. "You are at risk if you venture out far, into the countryside or the town, and more from ordinary assassins than from sorcery."

"Ah, well, 'tis good then, my friend, that you taught me how to use a sword."

~ ~ ~

"I wish you had arrived in time for the Autumn Feast! It is so solemn and dreary here compared to the celebrations in Sharsh."

"The equinox is considered a holy day, Lomela, all about the balance between light and dark. You have been here long enough and seen enough of our Kamatian ways to know that." Donzalo leaned back and looked about the familiar yet seemingly new room. Wasn't it much the same, really, the balcony, the faded tapestries, the young woman, as lovely as ever he remembered her? Yet he sensed it had changed.

"And you also know we celebrate Harvest Feast with a great deal of enthusiasm!"

"Oh, you Lamans are like children at Harvest Feast, with your masks and ghost stories and your feasting and dancing all night."

"Not so much dancing for you this year."

The princess sobered. "It is Bolos's, of course."

Donzalos nodded.

"He has become – better. Oh, he is still Bolos but I think all that happened this spring past awakened something in him. I have tried," she continued, staring at the floor before lifting her eyes to her companion, "to be a good wife to him."

"His drinking?"

"He gave up completely!" laughed Lomela. "He drinks only some brew of burnt barley that he learned of from our Siphic doctor."

Donzalo thought upon these things for a while. "It's all to the good, isn't it?" he finally said.

"I think so," replied the girl he had loved.

The cool air blew in from the balcony. There was touch of dampness to it, a harbinger of the cold coming.

~ ~ ~

"Damn this rain!"

"That's Laman weather for you, Lector. I've traveled this road in worse."

"Is it bad in winter, Blen?" Jobareth readjusted the soggy cloak he had pulled over his head.

"Not much snow this far south. That's why the Mountain Keep is where it is – it's the northernmost pass that remains open all winter." He thought a moment, then added, "Most winters."

"Ha, depending on what happens most times has often gotten people into trouble."

"Indeed. Most of the time!" Both men laughed. They had been cool when they met but had grown to like and even depend on each other. Weeks together on the road may do that – or create enemies.

"Without this mud we'd have been inside, before a fire by now."

"Ho, here is the turning of the road." He gestured to the men to follow him. "We'll find your fire shortly."

A few minutes later, the party stood before Castle Rosam's outermost gate.

5

Two men slid along a back street of Ros-town. "It's right up here," said the shorter of the pair.

His companion turned a round, pock-marked face to him. "What good will this do us?"

"The young Laman is likely to visit sooner or later. It's our best chance of catching him on the streets. Unless," he spat into the mud, "you want to risk waiting around the castle for him to come out."

"Good enough. He's a friend of the envoy, eh?"

"Yeah. I heard they arrived last night. Staying at the castle now but they'll move in down here in a day or two. There is the place." They had reached the end of an alley and he gestured to a large two-storied house on the far side of the street.

"Nice digs."

The shorter man, a dark broadly built fellow, nodded. "One of us will have to keep watch here from now on."

"Not from right now," replied the other, with a grin. "We can wait till someone moves in over there, right? Let's go grab an ale."

"Only one, though. We need to stay sharp."

"Of course. I'm not new to this business."

~ ~ ~

"So, my father is finished with you?"

"He is, friend Donzalo. Considering all that occurred last time I visited, he was surprisingly cordial."

"The count knows I consider you an ally."

Jobareth made a slight grimace at the use of the word. "An ally – I suppose so, for now, and ever a friend. But I have loyalties to my king," he paused, "and to his daughter. If our ends diverge, I will choose them, you know."

"None to Radal?"

"Only so far as he serves my king. I feel no personal loyalty to the man."

"As long as you put your loyalty to Lomela above that to Lareth, we will have no quarrels." Donzalo changed subject and tone. "How has it been with you this past six-month, Lector?"

"The existence of a very junior diplomat largely consists of copying out dispatches or taking dictation. At least, in the capital there are theaters to help break the boredom."

"We hear tales of the parties and fetes of the noble families, not to mention the royal court. Aren't you invited to those?"

"I am not noble, Donzalo. I am of a family of wine merchants." Jobareth laughed. "Although my grandfather could buy and sell most of the noblemen. Indeed, perhaps he already has, considering how much money he has lent them." Turning more serious, he continued. "I have always been welcome in the King's home, as my family's money has often been put in his service.

"And, someday, if I rise in the diplomatic corps, I may well be awarded a title. I will never be a member of the old aristocracy, however, and they will always snub me."

"Few noble families here go back more than three generations," mused Donzalo. "They were leaders in the wars against the Ani who became the new rulers when things settled down."

"One could say the same about our Sharsh royals," replied Jobareth. "Well, here we are. Shall I knock?"

"In a moment. You should know that my grandmother has not been well. She is an old woman, after all, but I never noticed it so much until my return."

Jobareth nodded. He had lost both his grandmothers in recent years. He turned and lightly rapped on the door.

Donzalo was slightly surprised, and perhaps even a bit pleased, that the same maid answered as on his last visit.

With mock solemnity, he proclaimed, "Lector Jobareth Nafal and Master Donzalo Rosam most humbly request audience with the Lady Vibola." The girl blushed and giggled at this, which pleased the young man even more. Jobareth glanced at her and, for a moment, thought he might know her from somewhere else.

Then she pulled open wide the door for their admittance. The

Countess seemed in better health and spirits than when last Donzalo had seen her, but still showed her age. Jobareth stepped forward and, bowing, kissed her hand. "My Lady Vibola."

"Oh, you're the young gallant with the book of poems. I remember you, sir! Why have you not come visit me for so long?" she added in a slightly peevish tone.

"Only duties abroad could keep me from your presence, my lady."

Vibola looked to the Lady Lomela, seated nearby. "Well, I couldn't rattle him. You were right, Granddaughter." Then both burst into laughter.

"Grandmother is up to her old tricks," Donzalo confided to his companion.

With a gracious smile, Jobareth turned to the princess. "My Lady Lomela. *You* remember, don't you?"

In answer, she rose to her feet and embraced her childhood friend. "I, too, wish you could have visited sooner."

"Well, my ladies, you will be putting up with me all winter, it seems. I may reside in the town but I shall spend much time here.

"Oh," he said, reaching into his pouch, "and I have a new book of poetry for you."

~ ~ ~

Two horses, two riders. On a dark and barely discernible pathway through the woods, Perdos and Sojel met.

"What news?" asked the Laman.

"None."

Perdos, by this time, knew better than to be offended by Sojel's taciturnity. This did not mean that he despised the man any the less.

"Then why are we meeting?"

"My men may or may not succeed in their mission. That is none of your concern. I need you to keep an eye on Paren's keep and the road between it and Castle Rosam."

"In case things do not go well." Perdos had learned to read between this Muram's lines.

Sojel stared impassively at the man he considered his underling.

Perdos, of course, thought himself no such thing. He spoke. "There is always that chance."

Then, in a gesture uncharacteristic for him, he went on. "It might give you a shot at your Cuddonian too. If the boy is dead, we no longer care what you do to his protector – but until he is, we will not allow you to interfere and bungle. Now keep a sharp lookout. I'll send Vanob along to you for a report. Meet him here in a week."

With that, the soldier turned his mount and rode away, disappearing into the darkened woods.

~ ~ ~

"It seems a decent enough place." Blen turned to the agent who had taken this house for them. "Bigger than we need right now, of course." But, he thought, when Doufan and the entire delegation arrives it may prove insufficient. "How far are we from the river?"

The agent fully understood why the knight asked this. "More than a hundred yards, sir. No flood waters reach this far."

"Then, Master Marmoyo, why is it raised up so high?" asked Jobareth. The wooden structure was practically on stilts.

"Um, I should say they don't reach this far most years. There are always exceptions."

The Sharshites laughed at their private joke.

"Most years will do, my good man. We expect flood waters in Rostown. Lector Jobareth," Blen asked his co-commander, "have you any objections to the house?"

"None. I was mostly concerned with it having an impressive front in a prestigious neighborhood. If there be such here. We can start moving in immediately."

"We'll need furnishings. Perhaps you can help us with that," Blen said, addressing the agent.

"Of course, sirs, of course. And I should say that this is as good a street as any in town and close to the largest lending houses."

"We shall prepare a list for you." He turned from the man and in a lowered voice asked, "Say, Jobareth, have you noticed the lurker across the street?"

"I can't say that I did. You are a more observant man than I." He glanced toward the opposite alley but saw no one. "Do you suspect trouble?"

"Possibly just a curious neighbor. Possibly something more. It's hard to tell," he said dryly, "most of the time."

6

"So, they celebrate tomorrow, a harvest feast of some sort." Moonface was explaining something to his partner, as they sat in a darkened corner of the ale-house, hidden from the eyes of a handful of patrons. Neither used proper names, being old to their game of espionage and murder, and wishing to leave no traces of themselves.

"We had harvest feasts back home," replied his comrade. "I think they have them about everywhere."

"But here they make something more of it. And they wear masks."

"Masks?" The idea of lawfully going disguised appealed to both.

"Aye. If our target comes down to celebrate, we can do our job and get out without anyone seeing our faces."

The shorter man nodded, then had a thought. "Ah, but what if Do – er, the target wears a mask as well?" He had nearly forgotten to leave all names out of the business. No one need overhear them mention the young Rosam.

"Are you jesting?" asked his round-faced companion. "He stands head and shoulders above just about everyone else in town! Besides," he confided, "our spy in the castle can point him out."

~ ~ ~

"You are joining us, Master Grippo?"

The young acolyte sprawled in a comfortable chair, his white robe – for only priests added red to their raiments – thrown open to reveal the costume of a jester. "I would not miss it. Harvest Feast is my favorite time of year."

Guesare gave forth a grunt of obvious disapproval. "Our minstrel," observed Donzalo, "is a player in a perpetual masque. To attend ours is rather redundant."

"Yet attend I shall, to keep an eye on you. I disapprove of you going into town, especially on such a night as this. As does," he observed, "your father."

Donzalo looked momentarily uncomfortable, knowing he should exercise more prudence. But he wanted out of this castle! It had been bad enough having a pair of guardsmen follow him about all summer.

"There will be a group of us," Grippo pointed out. "If we stick together, who would give us any trouble?" He was quite unaware of the plot against Donzalo, of course, and of much that had happened six months earlier.

"Ha! I would trust myself to the protection of Guesare far sooner than that crowd of foppish bloods."

The minstrel gave him a small bow. "Yet there is safety in numbers," he said.

Donzalo replied, with a shrug, "I don't intend to stay with them, anyway. We are going to the Sharshites's new place and will introduce Lector Nafal to the delights of Harvest Feast."

"Very well," spoke Guesare. "So Grippo here and some of his friends will accompany us down? A few men will help to discourage trouble, fops or not."

"A few women too, Sir Guesare," the acolyte said. "Everyone enjoys dressing up for the festival."

"Yes, and I have invited a guest of my own," added Donzalo.

~ ~ ~

"Now are you sure you won't be needing me, my lady?"

"I shall be fine, Traspa. I would have joined you had it not been," she put one hand to her belly, "for this."

"Ah, yes, Lady Lomela. I remember how you danced a year ago!" Traspa became uncharacteristically introspective for a moment. Something had been nagging at her for a while – ever since that boy Donzalo had returned, in fact. She would have to talk to her mistress later.

But now it was time for gaiety. "And you shall dance again, next year," she declared.

"That is up to the gods and my husband," replied Lomela. The thought of pregnancies – and their cause – led her to a moment of silence as well. "Have you a costume?" she asked, after her short reverie.

~ ~ ~

Elsewhere, another lady and her maid also conversed, but with much less amity.

"Should a young girl like you be out with that crowd?"

"Oh, my lady, Mistress Traspa is going along."

"Hmm, she seems somewhat sensible." opined the Lady Vibola. "Despite her dalliances with the kitchen staff."

"Food, I think, is more her weakness than men, my lady."

Vibola looked closely at her maid. This girl had more to her than she had first realized. "Posena," she said, "my grandson invited you, didn't he?"

"Yes, my lady." The girl prettily blushed but the older woman wasn't convinced completely of her innocence. She knew that there had come a tension between Donni and Lomela and that a woman with her wits about her might make something of it. The boy, at times, seemed a lost soul and Vibola wasn't the only one who could see that.

"Do not take advantage of him. Do you understand me?"

Posena nodded. "Yes, my lady." But she may or may not have meant it.

~ ~ ~

"It is a bother to take horses down with us," explained one of the young revelers. "The walk is not that far, anyway."

"It won't hurt you any to walk, Cousin," chided Donzalo. Guesare had not been pleased to find that they were traveling shanks' mare.

"Not on the way down," he admitted, "but coming back may be another question."

"No one goes home until morning!" laughed another of their companions. The minstrel recognized her as daughter to one of the knights in Borrago's retinue. "Except for poor Brother Grippo," she continued. "He has to be at his early services." She made a face at the unfortunate acolyte.

"All of you forget that the morrow is a holy day, albeit a minor one."

"Yes, the Feast of Family. It is observed in the Cuddon, as well, even if we don't follow your Kamatian ways. But we do not have this carnival the night before."

"Then that is your loss, Sir Guesare! What good is solemnity without some festivity to balance it?" The crowd murmured their approval. There were at least twenty of them, of varied station, and they had already started down the path toward town.

"Come and walk with us, Posena," called Donzalo. "You, as well, Mistress Traspa."

"Nay, young sir, I shall walk with Hendel here." She was hanging on the arm of a burly, bearded man in monk's robes. He was, of course, no monk but a pastry chef, costumed for the masque. "You go join them, girl," she told Posena, giving her a little push. "We can do fine without you." Traspa gave her companion a wink.

Soon, they were mingling with other groups on the road, some from the countryside, others come down separately from the castle. Many carried lanterns, carved fancifully from gourds or rutabagas, and others sang gaily. Posena walked demurely at Donzalo's side, not too close, yet closer than to anyone else. Behind their backs were many smiles.

7

"By Jov!" swore Guesare. "This be quite some party."

"That it is," agreed Jobareth, who stood beside his guests on the high porch of his new dwelling. Below them, the town blazed and blared in celebration.

"A warning, Sir Guesare," spoke Grippo, low and seriously. "It would be best not to use the names of the old gods, even in oaths. Some here may take it wrong." He had chosen to accompany Donzalo's group, parting ways with his young companions from the keep.

"Jov is still venerated in Sharsh," Jobareth pointed out. "You Kamatians are not so bold there."

"Your master, Radal, is of our way, isn't he? Even if he follows the Darkness rather than the One Truth." Grippo looked uncertain as to whether he should say more but wine and fellowship had loosened his tongue. "I do believe that there is one all-powerful God and it matters little what we choose to call him."

Jobareth looked out into the night for a moment and then asked, "Can you tell me, Master Grippo, why this all-powerful deity of yours allows evil to exist?"

"Because, my friend," replied the acolyte with a small smile, "evil is also all-powerful."

"Is this what the priests teach?" interjected Donzalo.

"Some of them," Guesare said. "I've heard such theology in Lorj. Here, I suspect, it smacks of heresy."

"Perhaps," agreed Brother Grippo. "So I usually keep such thoughts to myself."

Jobareth seemed intrigued by this concept. Ever the scholar, and somewhat a skeptic, he asked, "Then what *is* evil? Another god?"

The acolyte sighed. "I have read much on it and thought much on it. I would say evil is not a thing but, rather, the absence of good." He paused to gather together his thoughts. "And good – or God or Kamat or whatever name we choose – is the only reality. Good and evil are being and non-being, existence and the void.

"Can Being exist without emptiness?" he asked. "What would it fill? Nor, for that matter, could emptiness exist – if I might speak of the existence of that which does not actually exist – without Being to define it?"

Guesare nodded. "All well and good, Brother, but I have seen the work of Asak and know that it is more than real."

Grippo had an answer. "Asak embodies that part of Being which strives to return to the Void, to become nothing. It has taken form, even though it hates its form and its existence – all existence."

Posena had moved close to Donzalo and was hanging on his arm. Now she looked up at him. "I do not like this talk, Master Donzalo. It gives me shivers."

"And I as well," he replied. "Let us join the celebration, friends!"

~ ~ ~

Blen had not mingled with the guests of the diplomat, but he had kept his eyes and ears open. They had told him there was potential to this group of young people, even if they did not recognize it themselves. This was the sort of thing his king had sent him here to learn – not state secrets or military movements so much as who might move events, be it now or later.

He watched the party fade into the carnival lights and turned back to his duties. This house still needed much work. Marmoyo had scrounged some satisfactory furnishings, and the men had settled in. The soldiers were now barracked in a large rear room, which had probably been intended for dining. He himself had taken a space scarce longer than his own body, a pantry off the main room, as his quarters. It would allow him to be close to all that went on.

Jobareth, of course, had a bedroom upstairs, and the two servants were there as well. For now, meals came from a nearby inn.

Not that any of it mattered much. Their primary mission was to have a new embassy built above the town. Could it be readied in time for the ambassador's arrival? Blen doubted it. Not in the upcoming winter weather.

But they could choose the location – Jobareth said there was already a likely spot – and make preparations. Much of that would be Blen's task, as the young envoy would have to spend time on his diplomatic duties.

Jobareth Nafal seemed so young. Yet, Blen reminded himself, he was not much older. A soldier at sixteen, knighted before he turned twenty, he scarcely remembered ever feeling truly young.

For a moment, he wondered if he could slip on a mask and join the crowd without. No, he shook his head. It is too late for that.

~ ~ ~

Ever since he began shooting up to his current height, Donzalo had worn the same Harvest Feast costume: a tree. His reasoning for the choice? A tall man and a short man look the same wrapped inside a tree trunk. It was the best disguise.

Except that, by now, everyone knew who was in the tree.

So, for once, the young nobleman chose new costuming. He was advised in doing this, as well, by Guesare, who had pointed out the difficulties of wielding a sword while encased in wood. His guise was barely a costume at all, only festive robes and a half-mask, but Posena had told him it looked quite elegant.

That was enough for Donzalo. In fact, he had the tailor, already beleaguered at this season of year, immediately take time to make up a similar outfit for the girl.

The two of them wandered the carnival streets and it did not take long for them to go on hand in hand, ever more oblivious of their companions – jester Grippo, Jobareth as mock soldier in a bristling false beard, Guesare deigning to don a black half-mask and no more.

From a passing vendor, he bought them prani, the sugary, nut-filled candy that was known to every Laman child. Posena seemed oddly unfamiliar with it but downed hers with relish, regardless. Then she pulled his head down to her, pressed her sweetened lips to his. Her blond hair fell back, behind her pale, shapely shoulders.

Why, she looks like an Anian, thought Donzalo. Then he thought more. An Anian wouldn't know about prani.

"Who are you, truly?" he whispered to her.

"A friend," she whispered back.

Donzalo straightened himself and looked about. He did not see his companions; indeed, he didn't see anyone at all. They stood in the darkness at the mouth of some warehouse alley, shielded from the lights and festivities on the streets.

"Oh, watch out, my lord!" she suddenly cried. From deeper in the shadowed alley emerged two man-shadows, swords in hands. For a moment, it seemed she would stand by him. Then she broke and ran for the lights, barely slipping by one man who had moved to block Donzalo's exit, noticing only his round face, half-hidden behind a scarf.

~ ~ ~

Guesare turned to see a breathless girl running toward him. "Quickly," she gasped out. "Quickly, my lords! They – will – kill him."

Damn! How did we get separated? the minstrel asked himself. He knew this carnival was a bad idea.

Posena was running back the other way now and he followed her, Grippo and Jobareth not far behind. An alley opened to their left and from it came the sounds of metal on metal.

And in it stood Donzalo, calmly dueling with a short, powerfully-built, and decidedly skillful swordsman. In the mud, near them, lay a taller man, split open from gullet to bowels, the latter spilling out onto the clay. A scarf partly concealed his countenance.

Guesare bounded forward and the would-be assassin backed toward the darkness. Too late – Donzalo's sword flicked out and caught him even as he turned to bolt.

"Well, my large student has passed his final exam, I would say." The Cuddonian looked at the two dead men. "Still, it is fortunate that Posena was able to run and warn us."

Donzalo looked about. "Where is she?"

The girl had disappeared completely.

8

One masked figure whispered to another, then slipped away to rejoin the festival.

By Asak's hell, thought the other, whose costume was no more than a kerchief across his lower face, another plot gone awry. Who'd have thought the young Laman so capable?

And who was that girl with him?

But that was none of his concern. A courier must be dispatched immediately to the mountains with this news. He would ride himself, thought Sojel, but there was too much to do here, men to gather for his fall-back plan.

Sojel and his master always had a fall-back plan.

~ ~ ~

"I am sure she is Ani," stated Donzalo.

Guesare seemed perplexed and, for once, was quite speechless. He only shook his head.

"The question," Jobareth said, "is whether she intended you good or harm." He remembered now, too, how her appearance had seemed to touch at some memory in him. The Sharshite wondered about that but felt it best he say nothing.

The minstrel found his tongue. "If she meant ill for the boy, she would not have run to us."

The others nodded in agreement. "And," he continued, "even if she is Anian she need not be in the employ of the Empire. Spies will serve any master who pays well."

"Then a spy, you think?" asked Jobarth.

Donzalo replied to the question. "I would think so. Why else run away? She knew I had found her out."

With some reluctance, Guesare said, "Do you think we should inform the count, Donni? He could send soldiers out to search for her."

"Let her go. She did no harm and will not return."

The Cuddonian seemed relieved by the answer. "Probably so, probably so."

"Well, that's that. Are you gentlemen spending the night or heading back to the castle?"

"I must go, Lector," responded Brother Grippo. "I thank you for your hospitality."

"Any time, sir. I would hope to discuss philosophy with you at greater length, some day."

"Then I shall accompany good Grippo," said Donzalo. "And Guesare will accompany us, of course, as he feels obligated to protect me."

"Do not become arrogant," returned the minstrel, dryly. "The next time two skilled assassins attack you, luck may not be on your side."

~ ~ ~

Count Borrago did hear of the events that befell his son; it was inevitable that the town constables would report them. Of Posena, however, none made any mention. Donzalo chose to lie to his grandmother, telling her that her maid had been called home for a family death. His grandmother did not believe a word of it.

And she did not like her new maid one bit.

In a different room, Lomela was listening to her own maid.

"It was a dreadful fight, my lady! They say Donzalo was attacked by a half-dozen men and chopped them to pieces!"

The princess, despite herself – and knowing the story exaggerated – felt proud of her Donni, for there was still a place in her heart where he dwelt. "And Lady Vibola's maid was nowhere to be found?"

"No, my lady. Maybe they murdered the poor girl." The thought suddenly possessed her and Traspa heaved a great sob and fell to her knees. "Oh, my Lomela, there is so much wickedness in this world!"

She looked up to her mistress with teary eyes. "And I have done wickedness too. Forgive me, my lady!"

"Why, what are you talking about, Traspa? Come here and sit beside me."

"It – it was that Radal." The older woman slid onto the edge of

Lomela's couch and, reaching out, took her hands. "He made me do it!"

Lomela suddenly felt chill. "The Lord Radal has much to answer for." She spoke calmly. "Tell me of this, Traspa."

"It was he that had me spy on you and young Donzalo. He had me tell him things, bring him things. Oh lady, he said I was protecting you." Now the maid truly began to wail.

The princess pulled Traspa to her, wrapped her in her arms. "My dear, I know you would do me no harm. And I think now you know that Donni would not, either. Whatever that evil man had you do," she stared straight ahead, her face set in a bitter mask, "is more than forgiven."

Now her expression softened. "And Traspa," she said, raising the woman's head so she might look into her eyes, "from now on, serve only me."

"Yes, my lady, yes. You are my princess!" She began to sob again, head pressed against Lomela's bosom.

"Ah, yes, Traspa," the girl whispered, "there is much wickedness in this world."

~ ~ ~

Guesare was puzzled. An Anian spy in Castle Rosam? Well, that was not so strange; what was strange was that he would not know of it.

But then, there could be all sorts of spies here, or in the town. Some of them perhaps in Anian employ – though the Empire would be unlikely to send anyone of Ani birth here – or from any of a dozen or more other nations or city-states. Posena was a puzzle.

Not so much because she was a spy but because she had attached herself to Donzalo. To protect him? To corrupt him? Ah, for all he knew, she was no more than an adventuress looking to find herself a noble lover.

Such thoughts accompanied him all the way to the door of the Great Hall. Today was the Feast of the Family, the second day of Harvest Feast, and the only one on which people actually feasted.

Tomorrow, the Feast of the Dead, was given to fasting. Guesare had always preferred feasting to fasting.

He entered, and bowed toward the dais where Borrago and his family sat. Immediately, it registered on him that the Lady Vibola was not taking part. He felt a fleeting pang and felt as well that he should write an ode on the brevity of human life. Or, better yet, he could just go visit the old lady.

Borrago lifted a hand in greeting and went back to his conversation with his brother.

The hall was rather empty, actually. Oh, of course, only the family. There would be no guests, no diplomats, no retainers. A server showed him to a table not far from the count's.

Donzalo plunked himself down across from him. "Hail, Kinsman." The young fellow leaned back and stated, "And I am proud to call you such on the Feast of the Family."

"And I, you, Cousin Donzalo. So where's the food?"

"First comes the blessing of the hearth."

"Oh. We don't make a big thing of that in the Cuddon. For the head of the household, it is his first act of the day."

"Remember, we have priests here, Guesare. We have to give them something to do."

The minstrel smiled and nodded. "It's not that we don't have priests back home, you know. Not your Kamatians though – the old gods are still loved there." He paused. "And feared, as well."

"I do find it interesting that you hold to much the same pantheon as they do in Sharsh, despite all of Lama lying between you."

"We must be a related people, don't you think?" asked Guesare. "We even look somewhat alike."

"Here is the hierophant. We'll be eating soon."

The high priest entered, in robes of red and white – the more red, the higher the position in the hierarchy. Two priests of lesser rank attended him and, behind them, a pair of acolytes. "Hey, there's Grippo," whispered Donzalo.

Guesare nodded benignly. “That boy will be moving up in the world. If he isn’t drowned as a heretic first.”

The hearth, which was actually quite small, and more ceremonial than practical, had been thoroughly cleaned. Now the Hierophant opened his gilded jar and spread holy ash upon it, blessing it and the household for another year.

Then with a bow, the priest and his retinue exited.

“Probably wants to get home to dinner,” confided Donzalo.

“What family has a celibate priest?” queried the Cuddonian.

“Oh, the whole of the priesthood is considered his family, once a man is ordained. That must lead to a rather crowded table,” he chuckled.

“Here comes our food,” announced Guesare. “In the Cuddon, again, things are different. Most of the priests are married. And,” he added, “we have priestesses as well. They are not known for their celibacy.”

Servers came around with platters and bowls, filled with the fruits of the harvest and the hunt. There were sundry fowl, and beef and venison heaped up. Sweet Potatoes and maize were stacked, and bowls of light and dark gravies, and more fruits than Guesare could put a name to. He realized that he had neglected some aspects of his self-education.

“Very well,” he admitted with an exasperated – and certainly, exaggerated – tone. “The Cuddon can not match this.”

“And you brag so on the Yule celebration there!”

“This feast marks the half-way point between equinox and Yule. Six weeks or so – you really should come celebrate with us, my boy.”

“Ha, you didn’t even want me to go into town yet you think I should ride into those wild hills?”

“You might be far safer in said hills. Think on it, Donzalo. Think on it.”

9

"I need a full account of what has happened," said Count Borrago. He turned to his scribe. "You may leave. Have those papers ready for me to sign." The man bowed and departed wordlessly.

Across the table from Borrago sat his youngest son. "Just from you to me," he said. "No one else is here."

Donzalo gulped. It was not that he couldn't handle himself, but he missed having the support, moral or otherwise, of Guesare or Paren. "There's not much to it, Father," he began.

The count held up his hand. "We shall see. First though, I must say I am proud that you handled yourself so well. I – I long underestimated you, my son.

"Now, let's start from the start. You left here with a group."

"Yes, sir. There were several of us, to some of whom I'm not sure I could put names. But I was actually going down with Guesare and Grippo."

"And a serving girl, I hear."

The young man nodded a reply. "I did invite Grandmother's maid to accompany us. Oh, and Mistress Traspa was with her." He tried to sound nonchalant.

"I know. Mistress Traspa was the one who told me about the girl."

"Oh. Anyway, sir, we all went down to the celebration but I and Grippo and Guesare stopped by the house the Sharshites are renting."

"With the girl."

"Yes. with the girl. Who is, truly, the person you're interested in, right?"

The Count only smiled.

"All I can say is she ran off after the fight. And that she didn't seem to have anything to do with the assassins being there." Donzalo was not going to mention his suspicions of her being Ani. He spread his arms in a gesture of puzzlement. "Maybe she was just scared by all that happened and decided to go back to the farm."

"We both doubt that, Son."

"Or maybe she was a spy. Who knows? She's gone."

"She might not have been if I'd known of her right away. But you felt you owed her a debt, didn't you?" The count rose. "That's all right. She did run for help so I understand how you feel. I do wish we'd had the chance to find out who she was."

Donzalo rose now as well.

"Donni," continued his father, "we must decide soon where you will winter. Less than a fortnight here and you're already battling assassins. This is not good."

"I know, Father." The younger man bowed and left.

Borrago rose and walked to the slit of a window in this tower room. It was still light out. What if he went to see his other family on this day? Copago had a wife at home, and a pretty little daughter. His granddaughter. Would he be welcome?

Ah, he had papers to go over. Let them feast in peace and not be bothered by an old man.

~ ~ ~

Perdos waited beneath a massive oak, one of the wide-spreading oaks of the South, that overhung the road. It was time again for his weekly rendezvous with Vanob.

And here came the man, astride his gray nag. Perdos rose and held up his hand in greeting.

"What report?" asked the man.

"As usual," replied Perdos. "Nothing. Nothing passes on this forsaken road for days on end."

"That time of the year," shrugged Vanob. "I do have some news for your ears. Let's sit. I'm road-worn."

Both settled beneath the tree and the soldier pulled out a leather-covered flask, took a gulp, and offered it to Perdos. He sampled it – fierce corn liquor.

"Pretty potent stuff," said his companion. "The peasant folk around these parts brew it."

Perdos laughed at that. "I drank plenty enough of it down at Castle Rosam. So what is this news you bear?"

With something resembling a smirk, Vanob spoke. "The

sergeant's assassins failed him. That so-called boy has apparently turned into a swordsman and cut them to ribbons." He spat onto the dry leaves. "So much for his plotting."

Perdos saw that this man loathed Sojel as much as he. But then, who didn't?

"This means," continued Vanob, "that young Donzalo and his uncle may be passing back up this road soon to winter quarters. You'll need to keep a sharp lookout."

Perdos nodded. "Will I have more men to help? We may be able to set an ambush."

"Sojel himself will be coming soon with all the men he needs. Unless," he sneered, "he has once again underestimated his opponents."

~ ~ ~

"My Lady Lomela, this was among the dispatches I received yesterday." Jobareth held out an envelope to the princess. He knew its author's hand by the scrawl of an address.

As did Lomela. "Why, it's a letter from Fachalana." She tore it open. "Oh, her spelling is dreadful!"

"That was unlikely to change."

"Um-huh. Let me – hmm, yes – yes. Well, she does tell me to take good care of you, Jobo. She says she may find herself in sudden need of a husband."

The diplomat groaned.

"Hmm. Ah, wishes for a safe pregnancy – asking after my son – the usual pleasantries. And – well, this is odd. She asks about Donzalo. How might she have heard of him? She wouldn't – no, she wouldn't be part to her father's schemes, would she?"

"I would not think so, my lady." Jobareth asserted, coming to stand next to her. A knock came on the door, solid and rapid. "And speaking of Donzalo, that is most certainly he."

"Well then, make yourself useful and let him in. Do you think Traspa can do everything around here?"

It was indeed Donzalo, and Guesare as well. Both affected nonchalance – the minstrel better achieving it – but there was an air of the serious about them. "My lady," Donzalo came forward in greeting and lightly embraced Lomela. "Lector." He nodded a greeting to her companion.

Guesare gave a graceful bow to the pair and settled into a chair near the door.

"Well," began Donzalo, "it seems that I will be off again soon."

"Oh, Donni, already?"

"Yes. Pretty much everyone is in agreement on it – my father, my uncle, my shadow over there." He nodded toward the minstrel. "And I, as well. I can't just sit here in the castle all winter. I need to do something!"

"Not long ago you might have been content to read through the winter," the girl reminded him. "And visit with me and your grandmother."

"We all change." This came from Jobareth.

"I would that we didn't," replied the princess. "I would that we could be as we were." She, of a sudden, began to sob.

It was the Sharshite, not Donzalo, who put his arm around her in comfort. She raised her moist eyes to the young Laman. "When will you leave?"

"In two days, most likely." He gave Jobareth a look, as if undecided to continue in his presence. With a shrug, he continued. "You might as well know all this too, Lector.

"We will head back to my uncle's keep, giving out the word that I intend to winter there, but along the road Guesare and I shall part company with Sir Paren and head to the Cuddon. It is to be hoped that none will know where I am."

He looked to Traspa, busying herself on the far side of the room, but no doubt listening to everything. "Make sure this does not leave the room, Mistress Traspa. No gossiping in the kitchen."

"Traspa may be trusted," Lomela assured him. But the look she gave her maid was full of unspoken warning.

Traspa trembled slightly and spoke. "My mouth will be shut as tight as your father's purse, young lord!" She took a step forward and looked up into Donzalo's face. "And I beg your forgiveness for any harm I may have done before."

He pulled her into the embrace of his long arms. "All I ask of you, Traspa, is that you take good care of your lady while I am gone."

~ ~ ~

Blen and Jobareth, accompanied by a single soldier, trotted up the castle road.

"Here's the spot," said the envoy, pointing out a hill that overlooked their path. "Lord Radal picked it out when we were here in the spring."

"Nice piece of land," observed Blen. "Who owns it?"

"All the land about here, strictly speaking, belongs to the count. Even that under the house we currently rent. We would have to work out a lease with him and his agents before we could build."

"Will he want us so close to the castle?" asked Blen and then, laughing, answered himself. "Of course, he would be able to keep a better eye on us here."

"I know that he would prefer we stay in his keep rather than build an embassy. Both Lord Radal and the king are set against that idea. Hence, our current abode."

"It is an excellent location," the knight said and, dismounting, began to walk up the slope. Jobareth likewise alit from his horse to join him. The soldier came forward to hold their steeds.

"We would be about half-way between castle and town here," Jobareth informed him, "and near where the road to the great market splits away."

Blen nodded. "The view from up here is very good." They stood atop the rising, looking down toward the town and river. "I'm sure your master recognized that one could keep a watch on the road from here." He turned back toward the horses and their man below. "Not bad for defense, either, if need came."

"Let us hope it does not." Jobareth started his descent. "I shall approach Count Borrago on the morrow."

"You spend much time in his keep." It was a statement, flat and neutral.

"And no doubt will spend much more. It is part of the job. Still," he continued, "I enjoy the company there."

"The princess."

"Yes, and her friends as well. Young Donzalo is an interesting fellow."

Blen smiled inwardly to hear this youth describe Donazalo as "young," but then realized that he did hold two or three years advantage over the lordling. It was not unlike the difference between himself and Jobareth.

"I hear that he is leaving us."

The diplomat recognized that the knight was fishing for information. They might be partners, they might even be friends – though that still remained uncertain – but he knew that each had his own agenda, his own masters.

They had reached the horses. Jobareth swung up into the saddle and spoke loudly enough that the man holding his bridle might hear as well – he knew that at least one member of their retinue must be a spy for someone. "Yes, he is headed back to Sir Paren's manor for the winter. We'll see no more of Donzalo till spring."

10

So that's done, Radal told himself, as he watched the messenger bearing orders to his minion, Sojel, disappear down the shadowed hallway. But there is much more.

He turned back into his room, only to gather the necessary items – a book, a brazier, misshapen jars, the cask containing his greatest object of power – and then began to ascend into one of the soaring towers of Mountain Keep. Another magic, another spell that might bring him close to Asak's dark door, but must be accomplished.

All understood that this was the sorcerer's chamber, here high in this tower. No others came nor went. He shut the massive door, all of brass and ebony of the southern islands, behind him, turning an intricate key in its lock.

Sojel would be readying himself back in County Rosam, following the failure of his assassination plot, gathering his men to watch the road, perhaps even find the opportunity to attack the traveling Lamans. His sergeant had a larger force at his disposal now, a formidable troop, but that guaranteed nothing. Lord Radal had other servants to whom he could turn.

He laid out his magical objects before him, methodically, precisely. A breath before beginning; relax, he told himself. For a moment, he let his mind wander. Why was he doing this? Why did he continue to seek that boy's death?

And what if they had chosen to befriend him rather attempt his assassination? Ah well, that caravel had long sailed.

So far as he knew, Donzalo as yet had no son. That had lessened the urgency, led him to be cautious in his approach. And then, there was that gnawing conviction in him that it was all pointless. The oracle had spoken, hadn't it? He shrugged and set to work.

"I shall send the Rupa," he whispered to himself. "Yes."

~ ~ ~

Count Borrago was no fool. He therefore dispatched a dozen of his most battle-seasoned men to accompany Paren's small retinue on the road. The morning of their departure dawned clear and cold.

Donzalo breathed in the crisp air. “A year past, I might have been out gathering nuts on such a day.”

“I have consumed more than a few pecans since our arrival here,” said Guesare. “They do not grow so well nor plentifully in the Cuddon. But we do have filberts aplenty, thickets in the hollows of the hills.”

“It’s a dry country, isn’t it?”

“Not terribly so. The soil is poor, for the most part, which gives the land the look of desert to those who don’t know it. Much of what grows is scrubby. None of these huge oaks you have here.” Guesare’s tone had become, for a moment, wistful. “It’s my home. I love the high hills where only the wild grasses grow. In the spring,” he continued, “ah, in the spring they are ablaze with flowers. Who would give up such for trees?”

“A man who loves nuts, obviously,” replied Donzalo.

“Indeed, young friend, indeed. And a man who can not stay put in one place.”

The tall young man suddenly stood in his stirrups and reached an overhanging limb. “Here’s one nut at least,” he said, displaying the brown oblong he had plucked. “Now I can say I’ve gone gathering this year.”

“That’s no pecan,” said the minstrel, looking at the nut in Donzalo’s open palm.

“No, a wild hickory. Hard to shell and not much meat inside, but I’ll keep it anyway. A last memento of my home.” He tucked it into his belt pouch.

In a lowered voice, he asked, “How soon do we split away?”

“This first night, I think, would be best, with the cover of darkness. Paren will let the guard know of the plan before we leave – your father gave him a letter for the captain – and continue to his manor as if nothing happened.”

The Cuddonian looked up to the sky, suddenly. “What is it, Sir Guesare?” asked his companion.

"I don't know. I thought I felt a presence – up there." He gestured toward the heavens. "And I did not like what I felt."

~ ~ ~

Seventeen men, Perdos counted. Sojel had best bring an army if he intended to waylay these Lamans while they traveled. He urged his mount forward; if he hurried on the back trails he knew, he could ride ahead of the party and meet the sergeant and his men by morning. Would they attack knowing these odds?

He doubted it. There would be other opportunities after these soldiers had returned to Castle Rosam, when Paren's people would become less watchful, confident of their safety in their own keep.

If Sojel had any sense he would not let them catch a glimpse of him at this point in the game.

Night was come but a half-waned moon would soon provide enough light for him to make his way, even on these overhung paths through the woods. What if he just turned around right now, wondered Perdos, and sent an arrow towards that Cuddonian? Why should he care about the Sharshites and their schemes?

Best he keep to the set course for now. Opportunities would come. Forward rode Perdos, and eastward into the night.

~ ~ ~

"How long have you been on that beard, Donni?" It was an idle question, as the pair quietly threaded their way through the trees, leading their mounts.

"I stopped shaving the day we decided on this action. That makes this the, uh, third morning." He scratched at his bristling chin. "Or is it the fourth?"

"It is going to be a prodigious growth. None will recognize you."

"That was my thought, and that I might as well look like I belonged in the Cuddon." Donzalo rubbed his bristling chin. "Do you think we can ride now?"

"I believe so." Guesare glanced upward. "I wish that we had less moon, though."

"We both know it was better to go now than to wait a week or two."

"Oh, aye. I but grumble. Let's mount up."

"The moon may be of little concern shortly. Do you feel that southern wind?"

The wind was indeed building from the south. It felt moist and warm.

"Another autumn storm comes. Well, it will give us more cover."

"And slow us," said Donzalo. "How long yet is our way to the Cuddon?"

"Now that we have crossed the river, and if we held to this due eastward course, not much further than the one to your uncle's house." They had forded the Abam earlier that night, before the moon rose high. "But that," continued the minstrel, "would bring us only to the borders and no guarantee of safety. My home lies well north, in the upper Cuddon."

Within an hour, the moon was playing hide-and-seek behind the scuttling clouds. The country they crossed was rising, as well, and the way becoming more difficult.

"I will not chance a road yet," stated Guesare. "We can not be certain that our departure was not observed."

~ ~ ~

It had not been. Paren's company broke camp the next morning as if there were no change and set off up the road.

The road was become a lonely place, now as the year wound down. Many of the trees showed their naked, barren branches and the fallen leaves drifted across the pathway. But it was good weather and they were making good time; they should reach the manor by the morrow. Twenty-some leagues lay between that manor and Castle Rosam. Borrago's holdings were too far-flung, some said, and he should keep his brother closer.

Borrago trusted that brother to hold his border there, near the edge of the Cuddon, and to keep trade safe along River Abam. Not so much *on* the river, as much of its length was unnavigable, with shoals and falls aplenty, though some quantities of timber did come down its flow. The count's own patrols passed back and forth on this road, but rarely beyond Paren's keep.

"Captain," called Paren, "any report?"

Two scouts, sent ahead, had returned. "None, sir. No travelers, no tracks."

Paren nodded, as the commander continued. "But we both know someone is out there. All we can do is keep our eyes open and our swords ready."

"And let us hope this rain holds off," said Paren, glancing toward the gray skies, "so we may also keep our powder dry."

~ ~ ~

The first thing Lareth noted was how worn, how tired, his old comrade seemed. Magics again, he thought to himself. They will surely kill him and send him to one of the hells from which he now draws power. Where went that eager youngster he had taken under his wing, years agone?

"Here, sit, my friend. Bring wine," he ordered the attendant. The king took a chair opposite his councilor.

"You have taken measures, haven't you? No, don't tell me what. I neither need nor want to know."

Radal drank deeply of the cup he was brought. "I have done all I can, my king. All I can for now."

"Then that must be enough," responded Lareth. He gestured to a stack of dispatches. "Much has been going on in Lama."

This brought a grimacing smile to Radal's weary visage. "There is always much going on in Lama. Sometimes, I think we should just leave them on their side of the mountains and stay on our own."

"Were it only the Lamans, I might agree, Radal."

"Of course, of course." The sorcerer drained his cup. "The Coradeans and Partanacans both have their ambitions in Lama. Even the Ani, though no longer so much a threat."

"And in the mean time, I have to deal with the Mura on our northern border. They would like nothing better than a chance to reclaim Arolin from us. Ah, Radal, we should be old men enjoying our golden years."

"You, at least, are a grandfather, my king, and several times over. No such luck for me. Where is that attendant?" He held out his cup, steeling himself so only a slight tremor shook his hand, as the servitor came forward to refill it.

"Though, you know what, Lareth? My wayward Fachalana seems to have become interested in young Nafal. I may see her married yet!"

"That," replied the king, raising his own cup, "is something I will drink to."

11

"Afternoon is the best time for such doings," whispered Vanob. "Our sergeant knows the riders will be tired and sleepy."

But still too many and too wary for us to attack, thought Perdos. "We shall see," he said to his companion. Van seemed a solid fellow but the Laman did not forget for a moment that he was Sojel's man, body and soul.

They were in two parties, on either side of the road. A well-equipped troop, too, most with bows, a pair carrying matchlock muskets. These latter had dismounted, the better to aim their fire. Perdos had counted eighteen of them. Nineteen, if he included himself, which he did not particularly wish to do. They might be a formidable force to some but they did not match the professional soldiers coming up the road. Why, he himself could take on any two of them without likelihood of harm, bad arm and all.

"They come. Pass the word," came from the man to his left. He whispered the same to Vanob. Would Sojel order the attack?

He did not. The passing column of well-armed, well-armored men, shields all turned outward, was too daunting for ruffians accustomed to sure victory and the ambush of the helpless. The thud of their horses' hooves diminished into the distance.

Perdos smiled thinly. It had been as was to be expected. But there was something unexpected as well – he had counted the passing men and come up with only fifteen.

~ ~ ~

"That is a marvelous tale, my dear! I so wish I could have been there."

"I do not believe you could ever pull off the role of serving girl, Lana."

"It's true. I'll never be the actress you are."

"Nor have you the proper look. But I was not actress enough or the young gallant would never have recognized me as a fraud," replied the young woman. "I wonder if I should have dyed my hair."

"Oh, no, Maresta, you did right to remain blond. One mistake with the dye and you might have been given away – and you would have needed to keep dying it regularly. That's not easy for a servant in a castle."

"Especially one attending the Lady Vibola!" laughed the other. "Though I rather liked the old lady. She had integrity."

"The word that has leaked out is that they think you are an Anian spy," Fachalana told her. "That news arrived before you."

"It is a very long journey, even by the southern route. Did you learn of it from snooping in your father's papers?"

"No need. There are at least half a dozen young aides who fall over each other to whisper secrets to me."

Maresta smiled knowingly. "My Ani blood does show up rather boldly." She shook back her blond locks. "That is both a blessing and a curse when it comes to the stage."

"Oh, you were made to play villains, Maresta. Make the best of it!"

The young actress sighed. "Would that I had not played villain for brave Donzalo."

~ ~ ~

"Rain is bad enough. Is this typical Cuddon weather?"

Donzalo and Guesare pushed on through the sleet. "I am afraid so," responded the minstrel. "Be thankful we're on a road now. I wouldn't want to be crossing rough country in this."

The Laman thoroughly agreed with this. The last several days of cross-country travel, many of them rainy, had become increasingly difficult. "Does this road actually lead somewhere?"

"Aye, boy, it does. Follow it another hundred leagues and half that again and you can take a bath in River Siph."

"I'd rather have my bath in a tub of hot water, before a fire. Any such near us?"

"I fear not. Oh, there be cots about here, but no place we would expect welcome."

Though Guesare spoke nonchalantly, Donzalo suspected there

might be more than a few places in the wide world where the minstrel would not expect welcome.

"Well then," he asked, "how far and how long till we reach hospitality?"

"Seriously, my lad, I do not think we should make our presence known anywhere in this land until we are safely with my clan."

He paused. "Not only for fear of spies but for those who inhabit this land. There are many old feuds simmering in the Cuddon. And then, there are the Other Folk."

"I think this may be letting up," observed Donzalo, facing into the freezing wind. "The Others, eh? Trolls?"

"Aye, and various creatures of their kind. Most harmless, most willing to avoid us, but a dangerous folk, none the less." He also faced into the storm. "I think you're right. It may be clear by morning. And very cold.

"There is a place not far ahead where we may stop the night."

"Shelter?"

"Of a sort," laughed the Cuddonian.

The shelter of a sort consisted of an open log lean-to at the crossing of two roadways. "We will turn north here in the morning," said Guesare. "First a fire and some rest."

A fire already burned before the hut, the single figure of a man silhouetted against its flame. As they approached, he rose to turn and greet them.

"This, Donzalo, is my friend Oder."

~ ~ ~

Home! A weary Paren swung down from his horse and took a moment to look about. All in order, all as it should be. He felt weariness flow away from him. He had done what he could for his nephew and now it was time and enough to return to his duties here.

The Lady Thara burst from the door, and ran to embrace him. "Oh," she exclaimed, peering past his massive middle, "you have brought so many guests with you! Is – is Donni here?"

"No, my wife. Our Donzalo must ride other roads this winter and warm himself before other hearths. His destiny is no longer in our hands.

"But, yes, I have brought a fair number of hungry fellows with me. They shall remain here a few days before returning to Borrago."

Her eyes were full of questions.

"All will be explained," he told her, "sooner or later. Let me see to the men's barracking now and you see if you can prepare a large enough feast to fill them all."

The captain came up to stand beside him. "I believe I need a wife, Sir Paren."

"Well, you can't have mine," replied the reeve. "But there are plenty of other possibilities around this place. You'll be here a week. Make use of it!"

"Perhaps I shall, sir. I would that we could remain longer. I am certain that there was an armed band somewhere in those woods."

"As am I. Send out your patrols but if nothing is found, follow my brother's orders and return home."

The soldier nodded. "The count has ordered extra men on the road all winter. We won't forget you are up here."

~ ~ ~

"There is a fellow here, sir, walked right into camp. Says he was sent to see you – even knew you by name."

Sojel rose. "I expected someone. A messenger, it is?"

"I think not," replied Vanob. "He looks – well, I'm not sure how he looks."

"Bring him. No, wait, I'll go to him. Where has that Perdos gotten to? I haven't seen him around camp."

"I can't say I have either, Sergeant." The man rubbed his chin. "He rode out a bit after we made camp but I don't think he came back. Figured you'd sent him off to scout again."

"Deserted," spat the saturnine soldier. "He was never one of us, anyway – good riddance, I say. Where is this stranger?"

A somewhat plump individual, long beard spilling over long

robes, stood between two guards. He bowed, with surprising grace, to Sojel. "Sir," said he, "I am Sabatare the Mage."

Sojel but stared at him, saying nothing, but enjoying the man's growing unease.

"I – I am your fellow servant of – of the great – "

"Stop, fool," barked the sergeant. "Never mention his name before such as these." He swung his arm, indicating the band of scoundrels he commanded.

"Of course," replied the wizard, his face grown red. "Where – ?"

"Come with me."

He led the way past the pickets and then turned to appraise the man, looking him thoroughly up and down, the luxuriant beard, the thick middle, the soft hands. The robe, he suspected, would be spotless on a day of less inclement weather.

"You're Cuddonian, aren't you? And a wizard of sorts." Sojel practically sneered; he knew well what a real wizard looked like.

"My Lord –" He looked about before uttering the name. "Radal has ordered me to give you assistance."

"Ordered you? How? When? No messengers have reached me."

"Our master has messengers who travel far faster than men and horses, but only other mages can understand them. He sent one such to me last night."

Sojel nodded grimly. He knew his master used such at times. Then, another thought came to him. "He knows of what occurs here? Have you been reporting to him?"

"Not I, good sir," replied the wizard. "Not I." He leaned forward and whispered, as if in confidence, "He has sent the Rupa."

The sergeant had no idea what that might be. "Explain," he ordered. That was how one learned what was needed.

"It is a demon, a great flying shape like unto a bird. But not a bird," he added, barely murmuring, "not a bird at all.

"It has been observing the party of Lamans from a distance and reported their safe arrival to our master. Acting on what he heard from it, he sent his message to me."

"This Rupa came to you?"

"Oh, no sir!" The very idea obviously frightened the man. "Only one of his ordinary couriers, a little spirit of the winds. Just beholding the Rupa closely," he shivered, "might well tear the soul from a man's body and send it shrieking into hell."

"Humph. Well, tell me how you are supposed to help me with our problem."

An Anian! For a moment, a chill went though Donzalo and not a chill from the harsh north wind. Oh, he had seen Anian delegations at his father's court and even the occasional merchant come upriver from Morparas. But this was an Ani warrior, the villain of a hundred and more Laman folk tales, the savages who had looted and raped their way across his land scant generations earlier.

He shook the feeling off. That was another time and this was another man and a friend of Guesare, as well. He stepped forward to take the Ani's hand. Oder was blond, not surprisingly, far paler than a typical Laman or even those of Sharshite blood. And Donzalo found himself troubled by a seeming familiarity in the man's face. He looked like someone he knew, somehow.

"Greetings, young lord," said the warrior, with barely a discernible trace of accent. "And greetings to you, my beloved one." He opened his arms to Guesare.

Now Donzalo knew all about Guesare's proclivities yet he found himself slightly shocked to see the passion of the men's embrace. Oder winked at him over Guesare's shoulder. "This Cuddonian has ever been the sentimental one. Yet I wager he forgot all about me when we were apart."

Which Donazalo knew for the truth. "Let us get you two out of the weather," continued the Anian. "I've a warm fire and a pot of stew."

Sated with Oder's highly seasoned pottage and with their cloaks spread before the fire to dry, the world seemed almost halfway normal again to Donzalo. But this Anian –

He turned to the man and bluntly asked, "Are you a spy?"

Oder considered the question. "I can see how one might call me that. But Guesare here, now he is a true spy."

"'Tis true," admitted the Cuddonian. "but I only report to this Anian fellow. He took advantage of my innocence, long ago, and led me on this path!"

"It was he that corrupted me," protested Oder, "and seduced me to boot!"

Donzalo sighed. “How can I expect truth from a pair of minstrels? Why, making things up is your trade.”

“But we are very good at it, one must admit.” Donzalo wasn’t sure which said it and knew it didn’t matter. He was falling asleep and intended no other thoughts to intrude.

~ ~ ~

It was too late to find the trail, Perdos knew, and impossible in this weather anyway. Which night did the pair slip away? That would depend on where they were headed, he realized, and they could be headed anywhere.

No, not anywhere. They wouldn’t head toward Sharsh, so probably not to the west. South to Morparas, perhaps? The city was crawling with spies and hoodlums who would blithely turn them in for the price of a beer. Maybe to Tod-ford, though. Count Orgelo would be glad to harbor anyone Sharsh sought to harm – and use them for his own ends.

But no, Borrago would never agree to sending his son there.

Over the hills to the Siphic lands? Dangerous. But then, the minstrel came from those hills. Might they choose to hide there? Perdos exhaled slowly. A curse came to his lips. Of course. They were in the Cuddon and there was no way he, an outsider, was going to go searching through those hills for them. Best find some place to hole up for the winter and wait. They would come down to Lama again, sooner or later.

~ ~ ~

She was waiting, perched half inside the window. Red, she was, as rust, or as vermilion – no, like the hibiscus that used to grow by his mother’s window – and her wings spread like pools of fresh blood, or was it –

“None of your tricks,” Radal ordered, raising his hand in rebuke. She settled down, returning to one form, one subdued color, the color of old claret. “Report.”

"Maaaaneeee meeeeeen. Maaaaneeee speeeears! Aaaall hooome noooow." She stared at the wizard with eyes as blank as an old statue's. "Preeeeteeee meeeen. Ooone fooor Ruuupaaa?"

"If you fulfill your task, why not?" He very much enjoyed the thought of Guesare being carried off to service this creature in the far mountains where she nested. "So my force was not able to ambush them on the road." The Rupa nodded gravely.

"Well, we must crack the egg of Sir Paren's keep, it would seem. And you shall help, my lady of the crags!"

Still had Radal a clutch of hairs from the head of Donzalo, the work of the unwitting Traspa. From them, and from magic, he conjured forth an image of the boy before them. "This is he you must destroy, Rupa, to reclaim your freedom. Look well upon him and know him."

She stared, her impassive, almost beautiful, face giving no evidence of her thoughts. "Ruuuuupaaa gooooo!" she suddenly cried and launched herself from the parapet, winging eastward.

~ ~ ~

It was a wizened, waist-high creature that stood at the mage's side. Sojel had seen many things, evil things and some of them of his own doing, yet he shivered at the presence of an Other. Sabatare seemed to have grown more confident, regaining his poise now that he could flaunt his prowess in his own field.

With a bow of respect to his companion, the wizard excused himself – or so it seemed, for Sojel did not understand the tongue he spoke – and stepped forward. "I have gathered some, ah, helpers for our cause. This be their leader." He indicated the small man-creature behind him with a movement of his head. "A kobold. The Folk do not give out their names so best you simply address him as 'sir.'"

So that is a kobold, thought the sergeant to himself. Not so scary once you get used to it.

"It is – what? A chief of their tribe?"

"No, no, my good sir. He is not unlike you, leader of a band.

There be outlaws among the Others as surely as there be among men."

"Ah!" Knowing that made the little fellow seem even less strange. "How many does he command?"

"Perhaps a dozen. Some of his sort, an ogre – which is but an over-grown kobold, to be honest – a few trolls. Not that formidable a group but they can bolster your own men. And some," he added, lowering his voice as though imparting secrets, "know a bit of the minor magics."

"Well, keep them under control. If magic is needed, we depend on you." He looked the kobold up and down. "It looks tough enough, despite its stature."

The pair walked to where the fay awaited them. It – no, he – turned his face up, tilting it quizzically to stare at the sergeant. A long nose jutted from the thin, hairless face. Hairless everywhere, noted Sojel, as the little man went quite naked. Sabatare jabbered something at him.

This time, the soldier caught a few words and recognized that the pair were speaking some sort of pidgeon, cobbled together of Laman, Cuddonian, and who knew what else. Old Laman, that is, not the dialect of Muram used in most of the south these days.

It might be advantageous to learn some of this patois. Later. There were other tasks at hand.

"The detail from Borrago's castle is preparing to return home, it seems. We should be able to mount an attack in a few days." Sojel knew that the longer he waited, the less wary Paren's people would become. But not too long – winter was coming and he couldn't hold this band together forever. Nor would these Others be likely to wait. "So be prepared."

"Yes, Sergeant. I have, um, other news."

"Spit it out, man."

"Our master is sending the Rupa to join the attack." His small companion looked up at him in unmistakable fear at the mention of that name. "It has but one mission, to find and destroy this Donzalo person. It will not aid our assault but only seek its target. I would make sure," he warned, "that none get in its way."

~ ~ ~

"Stay, Madin."

The scribe settled himself back onto his stool. "I may have need of your pen," said Borrago.

The door stood ajar to this, the count's private chamber. It was a small room, one floor up, in the keep's central tower. Above it lay Borrago's own spartan quarters, with a narrow staircase connecting the two.

"Come in," he called. The Sharshite envoy, Jobareth Nafal, entered, followed closely by Sir Blen. Borrago remained uncertain on just what this man's status was – in public, he was reserved, at times barely noticeable, and seemed no more than an aide to Nafal. All the intelligence gathered by the count's agents, however, suggested that the two were equal in footing when it came to decisions.

The charade continued in their appearances today. The envoy was formally attired in a long Sharshite tunic, boldly colored green and white, and heavily embroidered. His companion was drab and could pass for a common soldier. Which he may well have been, once, surmised Borrago.

Formalities exchanged, the count went straight to the business at hand. Waving his guests to a pair of high-backed chairs, he settled back in his own and spoke. "So, you Sharshites want to build an embassy on my land, eh?"

"Yes, my lord," answered Jobareth. "If the chosen location is amenable to you."

"It's a nice piece of land," Borrago said, "but a bit far from town. Wouldn't you prefer to be down there?" I might prefer them on the other side of the mountains, he told himself.

Blen spoke up for the first time. "We felt that a location closer to your seat might be the better choice, sir."

"Maybe so." And perhaps it is better than actually having them in the keep, although young Nafal spends most of his time here anyway. "I have no objections.

"Now, as to the price," he continued with a smile.

"Sharsh is quite willing to pay any fair rent on the land, my lord," stated Jobareth. "We would hope to reach an agreement swiftly and begin building."

"I have had a lease drawn up." Borrago beckoned his scribe, who brought the document forward. Giving a quick last moment glance, for the Count was ever a meticulous man of business, he slid it forward across the table.

Jobareth read it with growing astonishment and wordlessly passed it to his companion. The knight only smiled lightly and handed it back with a nod. "You are most generous, my lord," said the envoy.

"Yes, it is my greatest failing," Borrago agreed, though not without the hint of a wink. "I have no need of Sharsh's money for that bit of land but I do want you to fix your residence and stay there. Hence, my terms."

"Despite your gracious terms," said Blen, "it will still need to be approved by someone back home. I think," he continued, with a glance at Nafal, "that they will readily agree to the price you ask."

"Oh, well, if one basket of groundnuts a year is too much, we can always renegotiate," the count replied. "So, sign the paper, if you will and we'll be done here."

Jobareth took the pen offered by Madin, the scribe, and scrawled a signature, and then again on a second copy. He handed it on to Blen, who did the same. So they *are* equal in this, thought Borrago.

The envoy then pulled out an official seal, the small sort a man of either diplomacy or business might carry on his person, inked it and stamped the documents. The secretary came forward and did the same with the count's seal and signed as well, as witness.

"I trust we can come up with the sufficient quantity of nuts for the next hundred years," Jobareth stated. "I should hate for my country to default on its obligations."

Then the young man changed course. "And with that out of the way, I will ask you to indulge me for a few moments more, my lord."

Borrago looked up from the freshly signed documents before him and then handed one back over to the Sharshites. "Yes?"

"Is there news of your son, sir? Donzalo, that is."

"Of course. I know you've little interest in the other one. Although," he added, "as a diplomat, perhaps you should.

"I received a messenger but this morning, newly returned from my brother's manor. All have arrived without incident. They even managed to stay ahead of most of the bad weather."

Jobareth knew that Donzalo would not have been with the party that arrived with Paren, and Borrago knew that he knew. This was a fact to which Blen was not privy so the two must need watch their words.

"Ah, sir, then please send my greetings and best wishes to your brother and your son. It is good to know that there were no difficulties."

The Sharshites rose and took their leave. Outside the door, Blen said, "I should bear that document to Sharsh myself."

Jobareth was surprised. "It is a long journey," he protested, "and certainly not the best time of year to undertake it."

"I know, Jobareth. There are other reasons I should return as well, and those I may not tell you."

The younger man nodded. "Each of us has his secrets. Try to be back by the Yule."

13

The road had not been so bad, at first. Frozen mud is not the kindest of pavings, and the horses often seemed about to lose their footing on the slippery surface. Finally, the three travelers dismounted and led their animals.

Alas, under the bright clear sky, the frozen mud soon became just mud, sucking at the feet of all six. The road led over ever steeper hills, slowing them further. “Never fear, boy,” Guesare told Donzalo, “we’ll make it home by the Yule.”

“If we don’t starve first,” grumbled the Laman.

“Oder is an excellent huntsman,” the minstrel assured him, “and we’ve money enough on us to buy provisions, if need come.”

“I thought we were avoiding those who dwell here.”

“Not so much now. There are larger villages ahead where traveling strangers are welcome enough. Even,” he nodded toward their companion, “the odd Anian.”

Said Anian responded. “Still, we shall wish to remain as inconspicuous as is possible.” He looked Donzalo up and down. “And to do so, we had better get this overgrown boy into some Cuddonian garments. He’s recognizable enough as it is.”

“None of my kilts would fit him, I fear,” stated Guesare. “Not without showing too much of what shouldn’t show.”

“They are far too garish, anyway,” Oder said. “We should get him outfitted soon, before he is seen.”

“I’ll slip into the next village by myself and buy something for him. A good length of cloth will do – that’s all a kilt is anyway – and then there will be no wondering as to why I might be purchasing over-sized garments.

“I know of a good camp spot not far ahead. What say we put an end to this day’s travel?”

The spot was, in fact, a shallow cave, little more than a depression in a rock wall, not far off the road, and sheltered in a small hollow, with a spring-fed stream trickling by. Its flow might well have been frozen earlier that morning.

Fire and food soon returned a semblance of cheer to the weary travelers.

"What say you bring out your rebec, friend?" said Guesare to the Anian.

"If you do the same," responded Oder.

For a few minutes, the two men exchanged random bits of music and brought their instruments into tune with each other. Or close to it.

"Here is a song of the Cuddon you should know," Guesare told Donzalo. "Oder and I often play it."

"'The Song of the Sword?'" asked Oder. "'Tis an Anian song, my friend."

"So you would like to believe," responded the Cuddonian. "In truth," he said, addressing Donzalo, "there must be hundreds of different verses bards have created over the years and no one knows where and when it started."

"Nor in what language, for that matter," said Oder, who put bow to his instrument and began to sing a plaintive yet forceful melody. His voice was surprisingly high and clear.

The song of the shining sword, I sing,
The song of a bird with a bright steel wing;
I sing of blows that make blades ring,
The life it has, the death it will bring.

Guesare took his turn on a second verse. As was his wont, he strummed rather than bowing the rebec.

My tales of time-lost battles I tell,
The sieges where great cities fell;
Of men who fought bravely and well,
The many souls sent down to hell.

The Cuddonian's singing was more emotional, less exact, than that of Oder, and he pitched his voice an octave lower. Donzalo recognized his technique as typical of the minstrels he had known. Oder took his turn.

To music made by clashing shields,
The sword sings over many fields;
A scythe Death unrelenting wields:
Men's lives, the crop his reaping yields.

"Is that one of yours?" asked Guesare.

"Nay, I heard it a while back on the northern borders. A bit of a mouthful isn't it?" Oder went on to sing another verse.

I watch by the light of a blood-red moon,
Where broken ramparts rise in ruin;
The cold wind carries a song of doom
As armies march to the ancient tune.

"Oh, that's different!" exclaimed Guesare. "Here's one of mine."

Before the sword, each nation falls;
It overthrows their high-built walls.
Barbarians plunder Tesra's halls;
The mighty end their days as thralls.

"Who is Tesra?" broke in Oder, lowering his bow.

"Rather, 'what is Tesra?'" Guesare answered. "Or perhaps more properly, 'where is Tesra?' You know of Tesra, don't you, Donni?"

"The legendary city of Tesra across the Central Sea. It ruled a great empire before the Mura took it." He pondered a moment. "And supposedly it was home to a race of mighty sorcerers."

Oder smiled. "Not so mighty if they let the Mura take their city."

"They were much fallen by then," said the Cuddonian. "So say the books, anyway."

He continued. "The books, or some of them, also say they were not truly a race of magicians, only very long lived. A people able to see their plans through. Whereas we may do well to see tomorrow."

"You try too hard to be literary," said Oder, pulling bow once again across his rebec. He threw back his long blond hair and raised his voice, and at that moment Donzalo realized of whom the man reminded him.

The sword cares naught for prideful powers
That gather wealth and build high towers.
It throws them down as mankind cowers;
They lie forgotten beneath the flowers.

"You have outdone me once again," remarked Guesare.

~ ~ ~

Things seemed quiet enough but Paren was uneasy.

He had watched Borrago's soldiers ride away. Their captain had done so with a too-obvious twinge of regret, as he left behind a woman to whom he had become somewhat attached over these past few days. He will certainly make other opportunities to visit here, the reeve told himself, especially if the patrols were to be increased along their road. It would be good to have such a man in his household, if he – and the widow Tiana – could woo him from his brother's service.

Did their enemies know that Donzalo was not here? Surely there were spies, if not worse, out there, and all this pretense must eventually be discovered. He could only hope his nephew be far enough away by then.

There was much to do on this manor before winter truly set in, the last of the harvest to get into storage, barns to repair, firewood to lay in. Best he back to his duties and put his trust, as always, to Kamat and to his sword.

~ ~ ~

The ferry slowly made its way across the Weldar, toward a fog-hidden western bank. Beyond it, Rosam holdings extended some distance and then various small-holders as the wide Laman valley rose toward the mountains. In those mountains lay Blen's destination, the end of a near two hundred league journey.

It would be a grueling ride, accomplished in less than half the time of his travel here with Nafal. Changes of horses would be posted regularly along his route, but there was no replacement for the rider.

He looked up the river. He could come back that way – a relatively short trip due east from the Mountain Keep would bring him to Oles on the upper Weldar and boats aplenty that could provide a leisurely passage down to Ros-town. Ah, if only he had the time for such a luxury!

It might not be a good season of year for that anyway. There would be ice on the river up there. Blen wished to dally no more than a day or two in the mountains, to deliver his documents to the proper diplomats and to closet with the king, who had sent word that he would be there for a few brief days.

Indeed, he might actually make it back to County Rosam by the Yule. He had no better place to celebrate it, after all.

~ ~ ~

There were men in the fields, and women too. Some were gathering in straw, the stubble left from the harvest. Some were in the barns and the yards, with brooms or with shovels. Children went about their chores or played hide-and-seek among the corn shocks. Some were moving animals from one field to another, or into pens, small eager dogs assisting.

None saw those who were creeping up on them.

Small wizened man-like forms crawled forward, their naked bodies daubed with paint. A misshapen creature, nigh as tall as a man but half again as broad, trundled through the forest's edge, a massive club in its grasp. And further behind, stocky, hairy little gray-skinned men, large of ear and of foot, whispered to each other, building up their resolve.

Elsewhere – on the other side of the manor, to be exact – men on horseback also waited.

Sojel blew his whistle, a loud shrill blast. He had been longing to put his lips to it for weeks, a signal for the death-dealing and cruelties that he loved. The motley mix of Others sprang forward and Sojel's men burst from the cover of the trees.

Some of Paren's folk turned and ran. Others turned to defend themselves with whatever was at hand. A pitchfork here, a pruning bill there; these were not a helpless people but the sturdy folk of a somewhat lawless frontier. Soldiers flew to their weapons, sword and lance and bow. A flash came from the ramparts of Paren's modest keep, followed by the thunder of a musket. One of the soldiers pitched from his horse.

The musketeer, naturally, was astonished he hit anything at such a range. He grinned and reloaded, hoping luck would again guide his shot. Then he felt a shadow pass over him.

Up he looked, where something moved before the sun. A great bird of some sort? He turned back to the loading of his matchlock.

Some of the reeve's garrison were on guard; some were out on patrol. Others were asleep. All were well tested veterans and more than a match for the rabble Sojel commanded, if they could ready themselves quickly, keep their attackers from capitalizing on the advantage of their surprise attack.

"It has come," Paren stated, matter-of-factly, to his master of arms. He had remained cautious, ready, continuing to expect some action, sooner or later.

"Shall we ride against them, sir?" asked the soldier.

"Only those who are already in saddle. The rest need to fall back and protect the gates. Get my people to safety before all else!"

The man nodded curtly and rushed to carry out his orders.

And far above, the Rupa circled, seeking the one she had been sent to destroy. He was not there. Wider the demon circled, and wider, searching. Higher she climbed, until the keep was no more than a crumb on the wide plate of the world.

Then she turned and sped north.

14

Hendel did not know why he was being called before the count. Had something gone awry in last night's dessert? Into the great hall he was led, where Borrago reposed in his high seat, the Lady Vibola to one side, the Lady Lomela to the other. All the faces here were stern, the nobles and the master of arms who stood below them.

This was serious. His portly frame shook as he realized that his secrets were secret no longer.

Borrago leaned back and took a long look at the cook, his distaste evident. Then he rose. "Hendel of Pora, I name you a spy."

The man fell to his knees in fear.

"I have my mother, the Lady Vibola, to thank for finding you out; aye, the Lady Lomela as well. And now I have this." He held up a slip of paper which Hendel knew to be one of the messages he had passed. "Thanks to their vigilance."

"Shame on you," cried the older woman, unable to contain herself. "You have used Mistress Traspa to become privy to our secrets!"

"She trusted in you," said the Lady Lomela from the count's other side. "She loved you, I think. That is a great betrayal."

"Hear my judgment," spoke Borrago. "Some would say you have done no great harm. Passed along a bit of gossip, an overheard confidence. For these I would have had you flogged from my lands. But I believe too that you betrayed my son and set murderers upon him; for this you should hang from my walls in the morning."

Hendel cringed in his terror, his bulk practically sinking into the stone floor.

"But," he went on, "my ladies have asked for clemency. Not for your miserable soul but for sake of our poor Traspa. You will leave and never again enter County Rosam on penalty of death. You shall tell Mistress Traspa that you must return to your homeland and duty will keep you there. And if you ever deal with another Sharshite, I shall command Sir Copago to hunt you down and return with your head." Copago, standing at attention before his father, smiled grimly.

"Now go and be outside my walls by sundown or you shall be thrown over them."

The two guards grasped the one-time maker of delightful desserts beneath his arms, heaved him up to stand quaking before his judge, and marched him out the door.

"Ah," sighed Borrago. "He really should have hung."

"No doubt, my son," said Vibola. "He could have been offed quietly and Mistress Traspa would never have known."

"Grandmother!" chided Lady Lomela.

"Just how did you two come to suspect the man?" asked Borrago, holding up his cup to summon a server holding a wine jug. "Do you want any, my ladies?"

Lomela began. "I had told the Lady Vibola of how Traspa unwittingly revealed things she shouldn't have. But Grandmother," she smiled at the Countess, "thought there might be more to it."

"I am a most untrusting old woman," stated Lady Vibola, taking the wine cup that had been brought to her. "This had better be your good stuff, Borri."

"So I kept watch," Lady Lomela continued. "It was not difficult. When she was not with me, Mistress Traspa was almost certain to be with that traitor."

"And we warned you to keep an eye on him and that was that," concluded Lady Vibola. She shook her head. "Poor trusting Traspa. But I'll drink to her loyalty," she said, and drained her cup.

~ ~ ~

"What do you think?" the one minstrel asked the other.

"He'll pass as Cuddonian if he keeps his mouth shut," the other replied.

"We rarely come this large," said Guesare, "but he has the proper look."

"I know I called your kilts gaudy, Brother – and I apologize – but you needn't have gone so far in the opposite direction."

"'Twas the only suitable cloth in town. I think it becomes the boy."

The 'boy' spoke. "It looks like a horse blanket."

"And it is," admitted Guesare. "I felt that gray plaid would look as good on you as on any steed."

Donzalo scrutinized his friend's face. "I know you enjoy your jests, Cousin, but I also know the purchase of a horse blanket was less likely to draw attention than any other sort of cloth.

"And speaking of cousins, what will be our relationship when we reach your home?"

"Not long ago I might have introduced you as who you are, my cousin Donzalo from Lama." He shook his head. "Perhaps not such a good idea, now."

"He could be an apprentice," suggested Oder.

"An apprentice who can neither play nor sing?"

"And how do you know that?" asked Donzalo.

"I heard you once when you drank too much," said the Cuddonian, "and thought you were alone. I was, um, with someone in the barn at your uncle's when you wandered in, bellowing."

Oder chuckled. "We have the better part of the day left. Let's be on the road."

Guesare looked up. "I feel something. A presence. The same as on the day we left Castle Rosam, Donni. Remember?"

The three looked out across the hills, drab in their late autumn cover, and to the misted horizons and to the cloudless sky. "There," cried Oder, pointing.

A speck, a mote, sometimes disappearing in the glare of midday sun. But growing, slowly, larger and larger.

"A bird?" wondered Donzalo.

"No," said Oder. "A dragon, maybe, though I've never seen one this far from the Lofty Mountains."

While they stood and peered upward, Guesare was charging his pistols.

~~~

Fachalana paced back and forth. She did so dramatically and
~~~

found herself comparing the different ways she strode across the room.

"Ah," she sighed. "I am the worst of frauds."

For a moment, she stared at herself in the full-length mirror. Fachalana had many full-length mirrors. She struck a stance and drew the saber that hung at her hip. Then, with an oath such as young ladies of breeding should not use, she threw the sword to the floor.

Would that she could go somewhere, anywhere, and truly use a sword. Not fencing practice with a shriveled old master who cared more for grace of movement than deadliness. She dreamed of crossing the mountains to Lama, as she had sent her friend Maresta.

"She may be a good spy but I would be one who acted!" she exclaimed, retrieving her sword from where she thrown it a moment before. She flourished it and laughed.

"Yes, the Lady Fachalana is a terrible fraud!"

~ ~ ~

"They've managed to close the gate!"

This was what Sojel had hoped to prevent. There had been a desperate battle before the gates, Paren and his guard charging like madmen to give his people time to reach safety. He did not care about those who were outside, a dozen or so of whom lay dead, and the rest fled to hide. The young Laman must be within those walls. Would Radal's demon help them dig him out?

His purpose here, he knew, was more to provide a distraction so this Rupa might act unhindered, but he would dearly like to take that keep, to sate all his lusts upon its inhabitants, to range through it with his sword until none were left alive.

He noticed a troll gnawing one of the bodies. Not one of his men – not that it mattered.

"What can you do about this, Mage?"

"There are spells," answered the wizard. "I prepared myself for just this eventuality."

Sabatare positioned himself well away from the keep, but on a slight rise so he might see the better. He surveyed the erstwhile battlefield, nodded to himself, and, raising his staff, began to weave an enchantment. Sojel watched him from where he directed his men.

"Bar sunai! Bar sunai set!" he commanded loudly. Nothing happened. The kobold leader at his side looked up at him, questions in his beady, deep-set eyes.

Then the mage lowered his staff, his face betraying his consternation. "I am blocked!"

A wizard, maybe a stronger one than he, had placed a spell here.

The little Other placed a hand upon his staff, to lend his magic to that of the mage. As one, they raised the rod and their arms and Sabatare called upon the strongest demon he dared to aid him. "Sebuchax! Sebuchax! Bar sunai set!" It seemed like a great wind rushed against the castle but the gate barely shivered, much less burst.

"It is no use," Sabatare moaned. "The protective spell is too well placed."

"Damned, useless hedge-wizard," growled Sojel.

The mage shrugged. "He who placed that charm is a gifted enchanter. 'Tis a simple bit of work but he imbued it with great strength. His strength, whomever he may be."

Arrows continued to fly from the battlements, and an occasional musket shot, mostly falling harmless, but Sojel saw a troll stumble.

"I think, sir," continued Sabatare, "that it is all moot anyway. I saw the Rupa circle yon keep and then fly far away. Your Donzalo must not be within."

"Now you tell me, idiot?"

"The trolls are running away!" called one of his men. The rest of the Other Folk broke and ran, following them.

"Fall back," he called. There was no more to do here and no reason to do it. He should report all this to his master, and soon.

But before quitting the battlefield, he ran his saber through Sabatare's chest and had the satisfaction of watching him gasp out his life. That's one thing done right today, anyway, Sergeant Sojel said to himself.

Oder sprang forward to prepare his own pistols. “Help me with the bows,” Guesare called, laying aside his readied brace. He and Donzalo quickly nocked the two powerful recurved weapons, and set the quivers up. Last, the young Laman pulled a small pistol of his own from his pouch and began winding its spring.

“The biggest man here has the smallest gunne!” laughed Oder. To Guesare, he said, “Arrows first, you think?”

“Yes, and then all together with the pistols!”

“What is it?” asked Donzalo, almost in a whisper as the great, red, winged shape glided down.

“The Rupa, I fear,” came the reply.

Oder swore an oath in his native tongue. It was the first time Donzalo had heard him use it.

Now, the thing swooped toward them. Was it a bird? No – or was it? And how large? It seemed hard to tell where it started and ended. “Don’t be dazzled by it,” cried Guesare. “That form serves to spread its terror but it must become solid to do us harm.”

The two bowmen drew their strings back to their cheekbones, arrows in readiness. “Wait for it – “ Suddenly, the Rupa seemed to coalesce, as if a lens were brought to focus. Both men loosed arrows and immediately reached for their pistols. Five shots rang out, almost as one. Did they have any effect on the creature?

None that they could see, yet it hissed and veered away. The minstrels took up their bows and reached for fresh arrows but Donzalo, in a moment of sudden inspiration, leaped upward, forward, all his lanky body and long arms reaching out, and threw his heavy saber toward the Rupa’s wing. It shrieked, and tumbled in the air.

“Go after its wings,” he cried, “and ground it!”

They could see now that their adversary was not so much bird as bat, and that Donzalo’s blade had torn the membrane of one wing. They could see also that ‘it’ was she, her body a deformed caricature of a woman’s.

She reverted now to her nebulous form, shifting colors and shapes that might dazzle and ensorcel an unwary man. It became difficult to tell exactly where she was at any moment, seeming to be on all sides at once. “This could drive one mad,” gasped Oder.

“Many men have become so,” came Guesare’s retort. “The Rupa entraps men for her own use, normally. This one has been sent to kill!”

The three stood, back to back to back, ready for her attack. It would come but would they still be sane enough to withstand it? Look away and she might take form instantly, killing claws at ones throat before he knew what happened. Fix ones eyes upon the Rupa and go mad, sooner or later.

But Donzalo thought he saw a faltering, an unevenness, in her mesmerizing flight. She was limping!

“She is hurt,” he said. “She won’t be able to keep this up.”

Guesare immediately saw. “It takes away from the power of her dance. And look, the ichor on the ground must be hers.”

“Can we outlast her?” wondered the Laman.

“We must, boy,” responded Oder.

And then she took form, a little above them, intending to pounce – to pounce upon Donzalo, of course, as she had no orders about the other two. Still, it might be nice to take a man or two back to her nest, back to her sisters in the wild high crags.

Again, she had misjudged the young man’s reach, or perhaps her strength had been oh so slightly sapped. He leapt into the air, slashing with all his strength. Down she went, her wing torn. Oder immediately swung and half-severed the other

The Rupa crouched, hissing. She tried to move, to start her hypnotic spell anew, but managed no better than a trembling double-image. “Weeel meeen keeeel meeee?” she wailed. “Ruuupaa liiiiike preeeteeee meeeen.” She folded her wings and wept.

Oder and Donzalo stepped back, uncertain. Not Guesare; he swung his sword without hesitation, decapitating the demon-woman. They stared for a moment at the head that lay upon the withered grass, at once repellent and somehow beautiful.

"She would have died here anyway, without the use of her wings," the Cuddonian pointed out.

~ ~ ~

"He left so sudden-like, my lady. I wonder if he loved me at all!"

"Who is to say, my dear Traspa? There are other cooks in the kitchen, you know."

"Indeed, my lady." The maid sniffled and then smiled. "And more than one of them has tried to get me away from that Hendel!"

"And anyone of them perhaps just as good!" declared Lomela.

"True, my lady, but none have his way with cake."

"Tell me," said the Lady Lomela, approaching the question cautiously, "did Hendel ever ask about where Master Donzalo was headed on his recent journey?"

"Why, yes he did. But I only told him that he was going to stay with his uncle. I can keep a secret, my princess!"

"That is good, Traspa. Considering how he ran off, you were wise not to trust him."

"'Twas none of his business anyway! He always snooped too much and gossiped too much about his betters."

"So I have heard, my dear, so I have heard."

~ ~ ~

In a small room in the theater district of Celatas, Sharsh's capital city, a young woman put pen to paper.

"Dearest brother," she wrote, "I am returned to Sharsh after my escapades in Lama."

That sounds good, she thought, and pushed back the blond locks that had fallen forward as she wrote. Maybe I *should* dye this. Hmm.

"It is regrettable that my cover was uncovered." She giggled as she wrote this, then went back to strike it out. "It is regrettable that my disguise was penetrated." Oh, I might not have minded Donzalo penetrating – no, don't think such things, young lady! "Yet it is fortunate that I helped prevent your person of interest from being skewered."

She thought for a moment, leaning forward on the tiny dressing table that served as desk, before starting again. "And it was indeed fortunate that my service here could coincide with your needs there. I never expected that attaching myself to the Lady F. might be so rewarding." And frequently frustrating. "Imagine her paying me to carry out her spy missions when I am already spying on her!

"I will be here at least through the winter. It is no time for travel and there is always work on the stage in this city, even if the provincial theaters do close down. And then, F. is always good for a little cash, if I'm short."

"I will continue to ply her for information and send that in my more formal reports. She does tell me much about her father's doings, and those of the diplomatic corps, in general. But she is restless and may not continue to be so reliable a source."

"Trusting all is well with you and that your tangled webs have netted a few flies."

She signed, "Your dearest sister, A."

That should do, she told herself. Then she thought of her handsome brother, when last she saw him. She must travel east again, soon. There was much out there that was important to her.

~ ~ ~

"I will soon take leave of you," Oder told them, as they sat their horses, looking northward. Guesare had known that but always preferred to make no mention of subjects he found unpleasant. "It has been good to ride with you, young Donzalo.

"And now must I be the Anian spy-master," he went on. "The Empire has an interest in you. We won't deny that. We know of the prophecy and we know of Lareth's intentions toward you. You may or may not be useful to us, politically, but we are always glad to thwart Sharsh.

"That is why we sent Guesare to you."

That minstrel had a slightly sheepish expression.

"So, are the Ani better than Sharsh?" asked Donzalo. "Why

should I trust you?" He knew well the history of the Anian occupation of his homeland.

"Our empire is grown old," said Oder. "We will never again come pouring over the mountains to conquer, as we did when we were savages fresh from the steppes. Now, we only hope to contain the ambitions of our neighbors."

"In other words," said Guesare, "a Lama free of Sharshite influence is to Anian advantage."

Oder nodded. "To the point, my brother, and quite true."

"Very well, that's out of the way," said Donzalo. "How much further to your home, Cousin?"

"Three or four days journey now, if the weather holds."

"Then let us ride." As the three urged their mounts forward, Guesare pulled forth his rebec and strummed a chord.

Oh, I shall sing the song of the sword,
Of that which ever is man's lord;
A song arising from discord,
For we march still to the song of the sword.

Afterword

This fantasy novel is set in a world and time of its own, although it most closely resembles 16th Century Central Europe. The stories and characters, the world in which they "exist," arise from ideas I have played with for many years.

I hope you have enjoyed this, the first book in the saga of Donzalo's Destiny. The story is continued in three further novels.

The poetry, incidentally, goes back quite a few years as well. The one here titled *The Song of the Sword* predates the idea of the book itself.

Stephen Brooke

~ ~ ~

Author and artist Stephen Brooke lives and works in an old farm-house in the Florida Panhandle. *The Song of the Sword* is his seventh book and the first novel in the Donzalo's Destiny series.

All are available from Arachis Press, a small publisher dedicated to presenting meaningful literature to readers of all ages. Visit our website for the complete catalog:
http://arachispress.com

www.ingramcontent.com/pod-product-compliance
Lightning Source LLC
LaVergne TN
LVHW090953080826
845145LV00003B/994

* 9 7 8 1 9 3 7 7 4 5 1 1 0 *